ANGEL in a FOREIGN CITY

FICTION

SUSPENSE

Some of the events depicted in this book actually occurred.
To protect the privacy and safety of his clients, sources and
investigators, the author has altered the names, places, times and
methods of operation. Any resemblance to actual events, locations
or persons, living or dead, is entirely coincidental.

BookSurge Publishing
7290-B Investment Drive
Charleston, SC 29418

CREDITS AND SPECIAL THANKS:

Hebrew Translation: Guy Tessler

Editor: Judith Kay Moore

Graphics: Revital Eyni

ISBN: 1-4196-7100-6
EAN-13: 978-1-4196-7100-5

In life, a person has to make decisions, even if they are not popular ones; however, he must always remain a human being.

Even though it has not yet been proven that there is life after death, I believe that you live twice, once during the daytime and the other at night.

(Moti Shapira)

This book is dedicated to my parents. While in my youth, they tried to encourage me to read books, while I preferred chasing a football and girls.

1.

"Haste is from Satan," states a well-known Jewish proverb, and that's how I was feeling. With only a few hours advance notice, I had to leave Los Angeles—my current home and the location of my Private Investigation office. I didn't even have time to arrange the necessary standard preparations prior to taking on an assignment such as the one I had been requested to complete.

When I'm asked to take a case outside of L.A., I insist upon lining up a guide, especially when it's in a foreign country. I look for a person with local knowledge who is able to make specific preparations prior to my arrival. Generally, this person gathers background information on the people involved in the investigation, and handles all of my reservations and accommodations.

When necessary, the guide coordinates with the local authorities; on more than one occasion they have enabled my team and me to avoid embarrassing situations without jeopardizing an entire case.

Not only was I unable to make those essential preparations this time, but I was also explicitly forbidden to do so. During our meeting the previous day, Rob had demanded of me, "Ethan, don't do anything until you have met with my man in Mexico City and heard him out."

Rob sounded very tense when he called and asked to meet with me. "I will be in your office in half an hour," he'd said. I had actually planned to spend some much-needed time with Meeka, a brilliant 27-year-old lawyer. This was going to be our last time together before she returned to Israel. However, I could not refuse Rob. He and I had known each other for over 20 years. He was my "other half"—my eternal partner during our five years in the Central Investigation Unit of the Israeli Police Force. We were together first in narcotics and eventually, in homicide. Our close-to-perfect cooperation on a professional level was forged by years spent together as brothers-in-arms. On a personal level, we were more than friends, yet no two people could be more different. I often believe that it is our differences that create our unique connection.

I am impulsive, and at times, fanatical. Throughout the years that Rob and I served together, I was even more restless, almost hyperactive; my style was to take out the bad guys immediately with no delay or hesitation. Rob, on the other hand, was cool. He would react slowly and with poise, considering all of his options several times before making a move.

We are also very different physically. I am quite tall and husky, with a fair complexion. Rob is short and skinny (although he has recently developed a small gut), and his features give away his Middle Eastern origin.

Rob has a great mind—extremely creative and complex, and as a result, he was repeatedly requested to take over the entire intelligence operation in the Central Unit.

Over the years, we have developed a rapport that

allows us to know exactly what the other is thinking or feeling without having to express it in words. We have participated in dozens of investigations in which we were required to spend days and nights together. Even after I married my girlfriend, Dianne, whom I had met during my military service, Rob and I continued to go out and spend off-duty time together. At times Dianne would join us, but usually it was just the two of us cruising the bars of Tel Aviv until the early hours of the morning.

"I am unclear as to why you married me," Dianne used to tease me. "You should have married Rob. He is a much better match for you than I am."

I would answer that the sex with Rob wasn't that great, and we would burst out laughing. In the beginning I thought she was only kidding; it was only later that I understood her complaint. It was not humor she was expressing, but rather bitterness and frustration over the truth.

Rob was the first to leave the force. The circumstances that led to his resignation were totally unexpected. All hell broke loose shortly after he was promoted to the rank of Chief Superintendent and appointed to the position of Deputy Commander of the Central Unit. At the time, anyone would have agreed that it seemed as though his way to the national command in Jerusalem was wide open.

We both loved the work we performed in the police force. The work we did was a true and much-needed public service, and we loved and believed in everything for which it stood. To our disappointment, a series of events eventually unraveled that belied our views and beliefs.

Rob was leading the Central Unit's investigation of a well-known business man, Aviram Melamedovitch, one of the more influential figures in the Israeli business scene with strong ties to powerful public figures. For some time,

Melamedovitch had been suspected of being a financial backer of a criminal operation on an international scale. We were tailing him closely and were certain we would nail him this time.

One morning Melamedovitch called a press conference at which he exposed the police surveillance he was under. He denied all the allegations. The climax of the event was when he revealed to reporters that the investigation was falsely created, intended to serve as a personal vendetta against him by the Deputy Commander of the Central Unit.

"The reason for this personal persecution," he explained, "is a result of an intimate relationship I had with his mother. After I refused his demands to stay away from her, he decided to make an attempt to destroy me financially and ruin my public reputation as personal revenge."

The press, always worshipping the business tycoon, was ever so critical of police activities, and had a field day with these allegations. The headlines of all the newspapers (many of them with business ties to Melamedovitch) showed Rob's picture on one side and Melamedovitch's on the other, reading in bold typeface, "High-Ranking Police Officer vs. Businessman Aviram Melamedovitch."

Rob had the opportunity to respond, but his statement was strategically hidden in the body of the article, and the damage was done. The story of the police officer harassing a public figure out of a personal quest for revenge was out there, and many people bought it.

The 'demon's dance' around Rob became very intense. I never doubted that the allegations against him had no basis in truth and that the notorious Aviram Melamedovitch used the well-known tactic of "the best defense is a good offense" to get us off his back. He threw slime on Rob, creating an uphill battle for Rob to fight in order to regain his good name and reputation.

When I think back on this whole fiasco, I want to believe that the whole thing was not the initiative of someone within the police department. However, Internal Affairs really seemed to have fun with this one, leaving a question in my mind. It was shocking for me to see the police commanders show indifference to the matter and allow Internal Affairs to garner headlines at the expense of a fellow officer.

My biggest disappointment was the lack of sympathy from our former friends in the Attorney General's office. We had always felt at home there and over the years, had established many formal and informal relationships. They succumbed to the mass hysteria and threw Rob to the lions. The treatment he received was disgraceful. Nobody was willing to go out on a limb and support him personally or professionally. Sheepishly, they all stayed hidden, waiting for the storm to pass. The lack of camaraderie of so many of the police officers in our unit remained an open wound for us many years after.

During my years with the police, I had met types like Aviram Melamedovitch who were able to influence the critical decision makers in the country. In spite of his power, I believed that at some point, someone would rise from the system and realize the great injustice done to one of the better police officers enlisted in the Israeli Police Force. It did not happen.

Rob's life had become a living hell. He was suspicious of everyone and trusted only me. Knowing that I had friends who were lawyers, he asked me to arrange a meeting with the one that I thought would be the best for him. I decided on a friend who had served in the paratrooper unit of the military with me and was now one of the most highly regarded lawyers in the country.

The attorney put it bluntly: "Your chances of winning this struggle are close to zero. You are slamming your head against a brick wall. If I were you, I would truly consider just going away and starting over. It would be better this way. However, should you decide to fight, I would be honored to be by your side."

Slowly, Rob realized that it was over. What was done was done. It was clear that his return to the Central Unit was impossible. Regardless, it took Rob almost a year to make the decision to put the whole thing behind him.

"Every second I stay here is a total waste of time," he told me bitterly. "I love my work, I love being a policeman, but there is life beyond the force. I accept that this part of my life is over."

The day Rob announced his resignation was one of the hardest days I can remember. Something inside me resigned that day too. I continued to function in the unit for a few more years, and became quite successful, but the police force stopped being a destiny for me, and became merely a workplace. That notion did not suit me at all.

"You've lost your spark," claimed my commanders, and they let me be. They stopped pressuring me to go to the officer's academy. Becoming an officer would mean more years of service, something I was obviously not prepared to do.

The only thing that kept me going during that period was my detective work. I received compliments and appreciation for the arrests I helped make, for solving a very complex murder case of a gay couple and for "impeccable functioning in a time of crisis" during a violent situation while chasing a gang of criminals on the outskirts of Tel Aviv.

Rob left Israel. Immediately after his retirement, he

moved to the U.S., received a law degree from UCLA, and became a partner in one of the most successful and reputable law firms in Los Angeles. In the beginning, we maintained contact, calling each other on birthdays and holidays. I even visited him once, during his internship, but naturally, we drifted apart.

A few years after Rob's humiliation, I also left the police department. I rejected all the pressure to stay, knowing that my departure was long overdue. The residue of frustration from the events surrounding Rob's departure from the force eliminated any remaining motivation I had had to remain there. I realized that I, too, had to start over.

The first two years on the outside were not very successful for me. I explored various avenues, leaving behind all of the violence and nightlife. I started a joint venture with someone I had met at a social event, and most of my severance pay was invested in the advertising of our company, using the remainder to buy a 1968 VW Bug. However, I soon realized my new partner was scamming me and I bailed out without looking back.

My personal life also hit a dead end. There had always been a little distance between Dianne and I. But now it had become complete alienation; we became two strangers sharing the same space. The birth of our daughter, Natalie, did not make things better. Eventually we separated. Even though I knew it was the right thing to do, it was a difficult experience, especially my separation from Natalie, whom I loved more than anything.

To recuperate, I decided to take a trip to the United States. In a downtown Los Angeles steak house, I unexpectedly bumped into Rob—a chance meeting that changed my life forever. I stayed an extra day, which turned into a week, and eventually, a month. We were like two fraternity brothers who had not seen each other since college. Night after night we relived our "good old days"—the stakeouts, the raids, the busts.

I kept telling Rob that I should go back home, but his response was always, "What's the hurry? Do you really have anything to go back to? Stay here and check out what this place has to offer."

What was here for me, so far away from Natalie? How could I get along with my rudimentary English, I worried. However, it eventually sunk in. Even though the idea seemed borderline lunatic to me, Rob was right. There was nothing substantial waiting for me.

In the beginning, I did a few minor investigations for him, as well as deliveries to and from the courthouse. My English improved rapidly, and within a short period of time (and a lot of help from Rob), I began getting bigger cases. Law firms and companies trusted me with their most sensitive matters. Slowly, though without a lot of effort, my clientele grew. My reputation and my professional abilities became better known across the country; my clients got 'heavier,' and so did my fees.

Even though I missed Natalie, I finally knew that I had found what I was looking for. The frustration that had been with me since leaving the police force—the feeling that despite my many achievements, I had wasted my best year—was gone, and it felt great. For the first time in my life, I could look myself in the mirror, or as my mother used to say, "look the bank manager straight in the eye." Even though I did not see myself as an American, Los Angeles was becoming my home. I returned to Israel only to see my daughter and visit my parents.

Two years ago, with Rob's encouragement, I leased a large office downtown, L.A., and opened "101," my own private-investigation company. Rob took care of the legalities and licensing. That explains why when he said, "I will be in your office in half an hour," he knew that I would be there waiting for him, no matter what else I had scheduled.

"I've got a job for you," he said immediately and sat himself upon one of the black leather couches. "It's big, urgent and in Mexico City."

"Mexico City? When do I need to be there?" I asked.

"Tomorrow morning."

"Oh, Rob, no. I'm sorry. I'm in the middle of two very sensitive cases and I can't leave town right now."

Rob shook his head and stressed, "You *need* to go. I don't know what's keeping you busy right now, or what you're not doing, but we're talking a *huge* payday."

"Which means?" I asked with amusement, and indeed, some curiosity.

Rob kept a straight and severe expression on his face.

"Exactly the way it sounds, as opposed to what you usually charge in your small and medium cases. We're not talking hundreds or thousands. You can name any price and you will get it. All expenses are on us, and if you get the job done, there will also be a very nice bonus. You have my word on it."

Ever since I opened the company, money had never been the main consideration when I accepted or rejected a case. I had struggled to end each year in the black. There were very few cases that left me with a really substantial profit. Usually, the financial costs, and especially the mental investment in each and every case, were not reflected adequately in the bottom line. The biggest benefit from all of these cases was the valuable contacts I made in the process. It's true that friends don't pay your bills, but today's connections can lead to a contact who allows you access to ordinarily unreachable places, and one day they might pay off big. At least, this is my rationale.

The possibility of making a large profit in a short period of time that would allow me to upgrade my life and company was very intriguing to say the least. It's true that the last thing on my mind was leaving Los Angeles right away. My girlfriend, Meeka, was about to return to Israel, and I wanted to be with her for the few days we had left.

She had arrived for a visit only a few months ago. However, during that time we had become very close companions indeed. What started as an innocent flirtation had become, at least from my point of view, a great love story. She would say repeatedly, "Don't raise your expectations, my dear, because this is as good as it's going to get." Regardless, it was clear to me that even for her, it was more than just a summer love—a lot more.

In the short period of time we were together, Meeka was able to shatter not only my daily routines, but also make me question my enduring and content bachelorhood. After the last few years of pleasurable temporary relationships with dozens of women, the attraction of home, family and children started tugging at my heart.

Meeka and I had agreed never to talk about a future together since she was returning to the only place in the world she wanted to live: Israel. So though we decided to enjoy the pleasures of the moment, it was clear to me that I did not want to give her up. Surrendering the precious little time we had left together was incomprehensible to me.

Even so, I asked Rob, "What are we talking about anyway?"

"Kidnapping of a little girl."

His face was even gloomier than before.

"A very important client of mine, his youngest daughter. He is one of the richest and most influential people in Mexico City. She was kidnapped by a professional group of criminals and they are asking for a ransom of nine million dollars."

You didn't have to be a Wall Street wizard to do the math. If they are asking for nine million, then Rob's client must have that kind of money. A fee of 10 percent of the ransom would be very reasonable, plus a small bonus of, let's say, a hundred thousand, and we're talking an even million. A million dollars! I had always thought that it was about time for my luck to change. I knew someday I'd get the case that would change my lifestyle to that of a 750 BMW IL owner—my dream car. Truthfully, even $10,000 for a week or so of work would get me pretty excited, but a million sounded a lot better!

"What about kidnapping insurance?" I inquired. "He must have *that.*"

"He has insurance, but he doesn't want to go that route. He's already had one incident where he's had to go through his insurance and they paid. He has other children and a large family. Most of his managers are insured. If he goes to the insurance with this case, not only will his premiums skyrocket, but he will be forced to increase his expenditures on improving security around his home and companies. The last time I counted, this guy had 22 companies, so just imagine the cost. He wants to keep this whole thing away from the headlines. If it comes out, others will try their luck and he'll become a victim of endless attempts of kidnapping and blackmail. Not very good for business, huh?"

"You're right about that," I agreed.

"Give me your OK now, and tomorrow morning a ticket will be waiting for you at the airport. You prefer flying coach if my memory serves me right."

He remembered correctly. I do prefer to fly coach. People in first class are usually old and boring business types, and all they do is sleep. A lot of good things have come out of acquaintances I've made while flying coach.

"Hold on, Rob!" I said, trying to resist his proposal. ('Meeka!' I thought.)

"Rob, you're not giving me time to breathe. I need a few minutes to see if I can put this thing together."

Rob put his hands on my desk and said quietly, "Ethan, I need you there. If you have any hesitations about what I am asking, then I am calling in a favor I believe I have a few on file with you, and I know you won't regret it."

I had to do it. This was Rob. I could no longer hesitate. It was no longer about the million dollars, about Meeka or about me. I just hoped she would understand.

"OK," I said.

Rob let out a sigh of relief.

"Great! The man we are talking about, Diego Valencia, is a tycoon that presides over an empire called 'Bartelieu.' This is an international conglomerate with dozens of entities ranging from radio stations, a fleet of cargo ships, airplanes, coal mines, all the way to supermarkets and drug stores. He is not a young man, 65 at least."

He went on to say, "When you meet him, you will find an honest and sensitive individual, with a lot of wisdom. He hates small talk and he is not open with strangers. It took me three years to have a conversation with him that wasn't business related. He is fanatical about his privacy and sees any stranger as a potential adversary. You cannot imagine how many hours it took to convince him to bring in help from the outside. We may have been given this opportunity because he's begun to suspect some of his own people."

"What do you mean?"

"I'm just going with a hunch here, but I have a feeling

he thinks some of his closest associates are cooperating with the kidnappers, maybe even giving them information that led to the kidnapping. He might tell you this, but he's pretty reluctant to speak about it, so try to bring it up when no one else is around."

"Understood."

"You will probably meet Jorge Cortez, a tall guy with a very thin mustache—can't miss him. He's the old man's right-hand-man. He's the vice president of the corporation and has some businesses of his own. He's married to Mona, one of Valencia's daughters. She's the reason he's back with the company. He quit a while back, but then failed miserably and got involved in some public scandals. As you know, in Mexico City, money talks."

"Anything else I need to know?"

"Yes. Make sure they update you on exactly what happened six months ago when Mariana, Valencia's niece, was snatched. The family and the insurance paid eight million dollars and received a dead girl in return. Maybe there is a connection between the two incidents. Oh, and one last thing: Don't talk about the fee. Leave that to me. All the rest is up to you. Valencia knows all he needs to know about you, and he is expecting you. I know you won't disappoint me. Good luck."

2.

'What a waste!' I thought to myself while my eyes scanned the huge suite on the top floor of the El Presidente Hotel in Mexico City. 'What a waste to be here alone!'

The suite was not presidential; it was ready for Caesar himself! It had a decadent aura to it, with an extravagant bed positioned in the center of the bedroom surrounded by four beautifully carved posts and above it was a gold-framed mirror mounted on the ceiling. Another mirror, just as ornate, was also above the jacuzzi which filled a large portion of the basketball-court-sized bathroom. As if that wasn't enough, the walls were decorated with erotic paintings, some of them quite explicit.

My mind went through the endless options that a room like this had to offer with the right companion. Again, I thought, 'What a waste to be here alone!'

As I predicted, breaking the news to Meeka hadn't gone well for me. Saying goodbye was not my strong point. She, on the other hand, with a studied indifference, pretended to not understand why I was feeling guilty about the unexpected change of plans.

"You have work and you need to do it. I have to leave

in a few days and I still have a million things to do. If you come back before I have to leave, that's great. If not, we will speak over the phone like two mature adults. We will say our goodbyes nicely and that's that. We knew this would eventually happen. We talked about it more than once. I will go, you will stay, and maybe, sometime in the future, we will meet again, or maybe not. So why are you making such a fuss over this trip?"

Of course, being a lawyer, her argument was flawless, but why couldn't she stop being so logical for one moment and speak from the heart?

Stretching out in the hot tub, allowing my body to be pummeled from all angles by the air jets, I was tempted to call Daphne. Once, four or five years ago, during a minor investigation I performed here in Mexico, we had some good times together.

It began on a strictly professional level. I needed a local assistant. A friend recommended her and gave me her phone number. She was Israeli, so I had no problem talking to her. She had no investigation experience, but she was a good student and quickly learned all she needed to know to perform superbly the role I intended for her. At first, I was so entangled in the case that I didn't notice how attractive she was. By the time I did notice, she had noticed me too, and we enjoyed each other immensely.

'Daphne, young and very curvy, you would fit well in this luscious place of earthly delights,' I thought. I was about to get out of the jacuzzi and give her a call, but I stopped suddenly at the thought of Meeka. What I wanted was to have *her* here, and no one else could substitute.

"When your head aches, study the Torah," states an old Talmudic proverb. "And when other parts ache, work and you will be healed," I said to myself. I had two hours until my meeting with Valencia. I decided to make the most of my time and read the general brief about Mexico and Mexico City that my ever-loyal secretary, Jody, had put together for me.

This had always been part of my process in any investigation. Before getting into the actual work at hand, I tried to learn, even superficially, about the environment in which I would be working. This is especially crucial when operating in a foreign country. My experience has taught me that a few key phrases in the local tongue, some knowledge of the most popular sports teams and the names of a few key politicians and local celebrities can come in handy. At least they give the client confidence that you are capable of operating outside of your natural habitat.

I opened my black carry-on in the middle of the monstrosity the hotel called a bed, and pulled out the stack of papers that Jody had shoved into my hands when we met on my way to the airport just a few hours ago. The first few pages had general information about Mexico, a country with a population of over 100 million fanatic soccer fans, 22 million of them in Mexico City. She had also included some basic Spanish vocabulary such as, "*hola,*" "*muchas gracias*" and "*por favor.*" The rest was pretty disappointing. It was information that would probably be more suited to a visitor wanting to tour Mexico and its capital and to enjoy the natural beauty and unbelievable sites of this country. Given the lack of time Jody had to prepare all of this, it was probably the most I could ask for. The only item that caught my attention was the statistics on the increasing crime rate in the country. According to the official numbers, the most common crimes are taxi holdups, armed bank robberies, ransom-motivated abductions, pick-pocketing and purse snatching. Not good if you live there or are a tourist. Another paragraph talked about a sharp increase in sexual assaults on women.

I was about to look for some more information on the Internet when my phone rang. For a second I hoped it was Meeka, but it wasn't. It was Jody.

"I am sorry to disturb you, but I need some urgent instructions," she said in a low, hoarse voice. "I hope you're not in the middle of something, like, really important."

"No I'm not 'like' in the middle of something important," I replied. With clients and staff she was always polite and professional. It was only with me that she loosened up.

"First, Jeanne and Alan asked that you contact them right away. From what they implied, they found the man we were after and are awaiting your orders. That's the first thing. Copy?"

"¿Sí, y el número dos?" I answered with the best pronunciation I could.

"Very funny!" she snorted. "Someone was looking for you from Guardian. They want to meet you ASAP. From what I understood, and you know I understand everything, they have a job for us."

"Tell them I am out of the country working on a case, and if it can wait a few days, I will be looking forward to talking to them about it when I get back."

"Yes, Boss. Oh, and one more thing. If I am not mistaken, and I rarely am, today is your birthday. So, happy birthday!"

"Thanks, Jody. As usual, you are not mistaken. I had tried to forget about it, believe me. I don't think realizing that you have reached the extremely old age of 44 is something to celebrate."

"I know a lot of 34-year-olds who would gladly trade

their youth for your wisdom...and, uh...body. Happy birthday, Mr. Eshed," she said in a Marilyn Monroe voice. "Oh, and one small request: Please do something fun today.

"Thank you, Jody. I'll try."

When I hung up the phone with Jody, I had to admit that I was happy someone remembered my birthday even though I was trying hard that day to forget about it myself. I realized that another year had passed and I still wasn't as fulfilled as I had hoped to be by now. When will I finally be content?

When I told Rob that I could not leave because of two very complex investigations, it was the absolute truth, maybe even an understatement. The first one was nearing conclusion, the other, just beginning to unfold. But oddly enough, they both had one thing in common: video recordings.

The investigation that Jeanne and Alan were working on was in its final phase. The stars of this one were two very well-known Los Angeles doctors who often graced the pages of gossip columns in many local newspapers. He was a plastic surgeon and she, a gynecologist.

The couple, young and good-looking, spent most of their time off work in their house in the Hollywood Hills with a breathtaking view of the entire L.A. basin. There, they spent most of the time in bed, but there was not a lot of resting going on. They were usually entangled in some form of athletic sex that would have tired even the most devoted follower of the "Kama Sutra."

Unfortunately, the couple wasn't alone in enjoying their festivities; without their knowledge, a neighbor had become an uninvited silent observer. As the previous owner of the couple's home, he had planted a few tiny, yet sophisticated, wireless cameras with long-range broadcasting capabilities in the house.

And so, every movement, every shout, every yawn, made its way to the neighbor's recording equipment and was immortalized on tape. It started as a hobby and then became an addiction. Within a few months, the neighbor had accumulated dozens of tapes displaying the activities of the couple. He watched them over and over again.

One night, his house was burglarized. A few weeks later, the couple realized that they had become popular hits on a few amateur-porn web sites.

A tape that was stolen from the peeping neighbor made its way to a porn distributor who made a killing off of it. The couple's attempts to get it off the Internet failed. All of the injunctions from the court and the publicity surrounding their battle turned the home movie into a "must-see" blockbuster. The distributor laughed all the way to the bank.

The judge explained to the couple that in order for the court ruling to be enforced, they had to personally serve the distributor with the court order. At that point in time, no one even knew who the distributor was. The guy was obviously familiar with the procedure. When word got to him of the court decision, he knew that he would be served and exposed. Therefore, he decided to take a vacation of indefinite length somewhere in Europe.

That's exactly where I stepped in. It wasn't an easy investigation. First, I had to learn how the industry worked. Who edited and packaged the material? How did recordings eventually end up on the Internet? I needed to understand who paid whom, along with the entire production cycle.

Eventually, I found the one who took the couple's intimate life and put it out there for the enjoyment of internet voyeurs. The man was one of the biggest porn distributors in Southern California. I also learned that he had fled to the Netherlands.

In order to find him there, I sent two of my best investigators to Amsterdam. Jeanne and Alan Davis were a married couple and as professional as they come. Jeanne had worked for many years with the FBI, and Alan was a researcher in the Justice Department.

The last I heard from them was that they had located the guy. If they asked me to call them urgently, it probably meant that the news was not good.

The second case was also about a video recording and, as in the first case, it involved sex. This time, however, the stars of the tape were a 60-year-old well-known, married Hollywood movie producer and a young, handsome male actor who had had a minor part in the last movie the producer made in Bangkok.

Someone caught them on camera making out and started blackmailing the producer, threatening to expose him on television and the Internet, and even to sell the pictures to the tabloids. At first, the blackmailer asked for 80 thousand dollars, and the producer paid. When another demand came in, the producer decided to put an end to the situation. I was hired through his attorney to make the producer's nightmare go away.

It was a very sensitive case that required the utmost discretion. No information could leak out. The producer made me swear that nothing would reach the press or the ears of his wife. My intuition led me along a certain path that eventually turned out to be the wrong one.

By the time I understood that we were off track, we had lost precious time. It was just last week that the puzzle was solved. It came following the work of one of my undercover investigators who was able to talk to some of the actors from the Bangkok production, including the young lover.

This kicked the investigation into high gear and was the key to solving the case.

I called the Netherlands. Jeanne's voice sounded crystal clear. It was hard to believe that she was half a world away.

"Jeanne speaking."

"Hey, Dear. It's me. Where are you?"

"We're in Amsterdam, a very nice city, but let's start with the happy stuff. Jody told on you, so happy birthday, Big Boy."

"Thanks, Jeanne."

In the background, I heard Alan asking to be added to the congratulations. Jeanne did so and immediately went back to business.

"Can I speak freely?"

That was why I loved working with these two. Besides being very nice people, they were also very professional and effective. That was the reason they were always my first pick for complex assignments.

"We're on my cell," I answered. "Is there anything new?"

"We've confirmed it. The man we have been following is the person we are looking for. Your friend here was incredibly helpful. Without him, it would have taken us forever. We have two courses of action. The first one is to serve him right away, but that means that you have to get here immediately. I know you like to do this in person. If you trust us with this, we can do it. I don't foresee any problems."

"And the second option is?" I asked.

"The second option is to play it safe. Learn his routine, and do it in a more orderly fashion, without rushing into it. However, there's a risk that he'll disappear again. What's it going to be?"

"We'll go with the second option. Take a few days and study him well. I'm not worried about you losing him. You know your stuff. I'm stuck here on a case, and I don't know how long it's going to take. It looks like you will have to serve him, so it's better if you find the right place and time to do it. Let's talk again this weekend. Prepare some alternatives, and we will decide how to do it. Have fun."

3.

Diego Valencia's ranch in the outskirts of the Santa Del Sol neighborhood was like a fortress. Security guards armed with small submachine guns were stationed everywhere, inside and out, from the electric main gate all the way to the large entrance of the central building. Some of the guards walked with vicious-looking attack dogs.

Valencia, a very impressive man, medium height and heavy-set, was dressed elegantly with his gray hair neatly combed back. He was waiting for me at the entrance to the house—a four-story affair.

He shook my hand with the firmness of a confident master.

"*Hola*. I am very happy to have you in my home. Rob has said many good things about you."

His English was perfect. His warm words of welcome, however, did not match his distant tone and somber expression. He gestured towards the door and invited me inside. He then led me through a wide, marble-paved corridor into a big room furnished with massive antique furniture.

"May I offer you a drink—coffee, alcohol?"

I shook my head, "No, thank you."

He walked over to a large desk surrounded by three comfortable-looking leather chairs.

"Please sit down." He sat while pointing at the chair opposite him.

"I really appreciate that you were able to come with such short notice."

He sighed and became silent. I could see that this was probably as much emotion as I could expect from this kind of man. I used the brief pause to study him closely. I saw in front of me a very impressive man indeed. His entire being projected wealth and honor—a tremendous amount of both. His face was round and serious. Set in a dark complexion, his green eyes showed fatigue, yet much wisdom and life experience. They had seen it all.

It was evident that the black, three-piece suit he wore was tailored from a fine fabric, probably special-ordered from a Parisian tailor. The watch on his hand was one of the best and most expensive of the popular "Patek Philippe" Swiss watches.

Leaning back in the leather chair, his whole demeanor was that of a master. Even though I knew an emotional storm was churning within him, he did not let it show. His deep voice and measured movements reflected control as well as self-esteem and credibility. It made me happy to see that this is the man I would be working for—a man to my liking.

"I want us to talk a little before I invite my son-in-law, Jorge Cortez, to join us. You two will work together on this matter."

"I don't know if Rob explained to you that the most important thing to me is that none of this will be leaked to the public. I want no one to know of the kidnapping of the girl or of the measures being taken to retrieve her. No one in this compound, except for the driver who was with her when she was abducted, is aware of the situation. I am afraid that one careless word could alert the police, which is the last thing I want. It's not just because of their threat to kill Carmen if we involve the police, but for other reasons as well.

He studied me, looking to see how I would respond; I didn't. He paused for a moment and then continued.

"I trust my people. I handpicked them very carefully, but even *I* can make mistakes. I do not rule out the possibility that one of my employees, for one reason or another, chose to act against me. I hope you understand what I mean."

I nodded my head in agreement.

"Mr. Eshed, what do you require of me so that you can start working immediately?"

"First, I need a complete list of all the employees in the estate. I need a list of everybody, with no exceptions, including the service and temporary personnel. Second, I would like your permission to bring someone on my behalf to work undercover?"

Valencia took a deep breath. "If you think it is absolutely necessary, I will agree. However, I fear this will compromise the discretion we discussed earlier. The seven to eight permanent staff members working with me have been together for many years. I do not think I can find a reasonable excuse to hire a new person, other than a security guard, and they are all under Cortez."

He looked at me again with a weary look. "I need you to understand that this is a delicate situation I am in. I need to be extremely careful. As much as I trust everyone, I suspect everyone. No scenario would shock me. This is why I accepted Rob's offer to put Carmen's fate in your hands. You are suitable because you are a total outsider. It should be clear that you work for me, and me alone. I am the one who invited you and I am the one who is paying for your services. You are free to do whatever you feel is necessary, and in return, I demand total loyalty."

Valencia noticed my slight annoyance and continued, "I apologize. Don't get me wrong; I have not for a moment doubted your personal and professional integrity. My trust in you is 100 percent, otherwise we would not be sitting here having this conversation. Rob vouched for you, and I trust him. I explained it the way I did because here, in Mexico, the rules of the game are different. You will find this out for yourself over the next few days. We play by the rules of the jungle. This is the way it is, but I do not want to elaborate on this right now. When Rob is here tomorrow, we will have a chance to talk about it further. Now, with your permission, I want to invite Cortez to join us. He has already made some attempts to track the kidnappers, though so far, unsuccessfully. He has the most recent information and will be glad to be of service and assist you with anything you require."

The first thought that crossed my mind as I was shaking Jorge Cortez's hand was, 'What a wimp!' It was his soft handshake, and wide, artificial showing of teeth. I assumed that was what he considered to be a smile. He was tall and skinny, and his whole appearance was one of submission.

"I hope your room at El Presidente is to your liking," he said with that smile of his as we sat down. "Alfredo, the hotel manager, and his entire staff were instructed by me to be at your service around the clock. So please, do not hesitate to use them if you need anything. Our management company, 'Paradise,' runs the hotel."

"*Muchas gracías,*" I mumbled, slightly embarrassed. "Everything is really wonderful. The room is great as well as the service."

"Above all, like Mr. Valencia has probably already told you, I, myself, will be at your service for anything you need and will be honored to help as much as I can."

"Mr. Eshed, what do you need from us so that you can get started?" Valencia's deep voice interrupted the idle conversation that Cortez was leading. "It is better to get to the point right away; we have already wasted a few days without making any progress. We are running out of time and need to take action immediately."

"I would really like to hear from you about what exactly has happened. The information I have is partial. I would like to have all the details that you have," I said.

Valencia reached for the cigar box on the coffee table next to him. His voice was calm and steady.

"Carmen is nine and a half years old. She is my youngest daughter. On Monday, four days ago, she left for school as she always does. At the end of the day, our limousine, driven by her regular chauffer and accompanied by a bodyguard, went to pick her up from school. On the way back home, the car was ambushed in a well-planned attack. There were four or five armed assailants. The driver and the bodyguard were wounded in a shoot-out and Carmen was snatched. That evening, the ransom call came in demanding nine million dollars or they said they would kill her."

"Where is the school? Where are the employees that were attacked? How trustworthy are they in your eyes?" I asked.

Valencia looked at Cortez.

"I will give you all of this information," answered Cortez. "Mr. Valencia does not have all the small details. I feel it is unnecessary to burden him with too much information. I suggest that right now, we discuss how to deal with the kidnappers and develop a strategy about how to respond the next time they call. We can discuss the operational aspects this evening over dinner."

"That's fine with me" I answered. "When is the next call from the kidnappers expected?"

"Tomorrow night at 11 p.m.," Valencia answered.

The next question I addressed to Cortez.

"Did you trace the incoming calls? Do you know where they are coming from?"

"The two calls that arrived so far were from two separate cell phones. We know the identity of the phone owners, and they both said they had lost their phones within the last two weeks."

"If you want, you can interrogate them or go over the transcripts. Mr. Cortez has all that available for you if necessary. Perhaps something was overlooked," added Valencia.

Addressing his son-in-law, he continued, "In any case, please make sure to make an interpreter available for Mr. Eshed, someone with excellent English and Spanish."

Cortez nodded while Valencia asked me, "Can I offer you an excellent Cuban cigar?"

"No, thank you," I answered. "I don't smoke."

"I prefer my own cigarettes," said Cortez without being asked and took one from a pack of Kent cigarettes he had in his jacket. He waited until Valencia lit his cigar and only then did he light his own.

I looked at Valencia. His tired gaze was focused on the tip of the cigar in his mouth.

"Cortez is right," he said. "I don't think it's necessary for me to get into more details right now, as he knows more about the situation than I do. You two will discuss it later. Mr. Eshed, by tomorrow night you must figure out what we need to do. What will we tell them? They will start losing their patience. In the last conversation, the man I spoke with sounded restless and short-tempered. They can do anything. I can only hope that Carmen is still alive."

His voice broke slightly as he continued, "To be truthful, I'm not so sure we did the right thing by not paying the ransom. When I think of Carmen lying scared in some stinking pit or warehouse, I am beside myself."

The room turned silent. Valencia's face looked tormented. He closed his eyes and sighed heavily.

It was Cortez who broke the silence.

"It's not too late to change your mind, Sir. I don't doubt Mr. Eshed's professionalism and his ability to track down who is doing this to us, but I shiver at the thought of what is happening to Carmen and what could happen to her if things go wrong. Maybe it is better to pay the ransom and be done with it, but of course, this decision is yours alone to make. I would urge you again to reconsider getting some help from the police."

Valencia opened his eyes sharply and gave Cortez a stern look.

As close to shouting as I would ever hear him, he demanded, "No! No police! No insurance either! I have already told you that this is entirely out of the question. The slightest police involvement means certain death to my Carmen. Do not mention it ever again!"

I listened to them in silence, trying to learn more about these two people and their relationship from more than what was being expressed in their words.

Valencia continued in a much softer tone, "You know very well that the money is not the reason I do not want to pay the ransom. I think that this time we need to catch these criminals. I have no doubt that the ease with which we paid the ransom for Mariana caused us to lose her. We paid eight million dollars and got a dead girl. What if it's the same people as the last time? Why should they act differently now?"

Cortez inhaled his Kent and replied, "You know we checked that already, and all the signs show that it is another group. They work in a very different way than Mariana's kidnappers."

"Right, you told me that," said Valencia with his head down. "Mr. Eshed," he addressed me in what was clear to be the final statement of this conversation, "from now on it is all in your hands. I will not take any more of your time. Do not hesitate to call me if you need anything. The safe return of my daughter is my only priority. Do everything within your power to make it happen."

4.

A short while after leaving the mansion, I was sitting in front of a computer in the public library at the edge of the magnificent Zócalo, or Plaza of the Constitution, where Valencia's limo driver had dropped me off. I planned to gather as much information as possible on Valencia's operation before my early dinner with Cortez.

From previous experience conducting investigations outside the U.S., I learned that newspaper articles could provide fascinating information on the persons involved in a case. Sometimes, even an item in a gossip column can provide insight into the personality of an individual, and lead to the revelation of a vital thread that may break a case open. Obviously, financial and legal articles provide much-needed information as well.

This time, it seemed an impossible task. There were an abundance of articles about Valencia. Unfortunately, they were all in Spanish, leaving me with nothing.

"Sorry, Sir; I can not help you," said the manager of the library's media wing impatiently. She didn't even bother to look at me as she continued to sort the huge pile of newspapers on her desk.

"I am very sorry, but we do not have foreign-language newspapers in our archives."

"I understand, but I am sure there is an English-language newspaper published in Mexico. Do you happen to know where I can find one...?"

I smiled at her even though I was ready to bite her head off. I knew that a smile might create some sort of connection. I guess her philosophy was a little different than mine because the big woman seemed even more irritated than before as she glared at me through her thick spectacles perched on her crooked nose. She did not even let me finish my sentence.

"Sir, I already told you. I will say it again and I will not repeat it a third time. Our archives have *Spanish newspapers only!*"

Her aggressive attitude left me speechless. I backed away from the counter and looked around, not knowing what to do next. I felt helpless, a feeling I hated. I stood, thinking about what I should do.

"Excuse me," said a gentle voice in English from behind me. "I happened to hear your conversation and of course there is a local edition of the Post in English in Mexico City. They have a very well-organized archive and they let everyone access it."

I quickly turned around and my surprise was complete. In front of me, I saw a small, good-looking young woman, wearing a colorful, flower-embossed, short-sleeved dress. Her stunning green eyes were smiling at me in shyness.

"I'm sorry, I couldn't stand the way that woman answered you. I think it is disgraceful and I apologize on behalf of Mexico. They wonder why tourists don't feel welcome here!"

She was beautiful, very beautiful. The sharp contrast between those green eyes, her dark-brown skin and her raven hair was hypnotizing. Instinctively, as a result of a disgusting habit of years, I peeked at her breasts which tightly filled her otherwise loose dress. The contrast between the luscious breasts and the petite figure was wonderful.

She smiled self-consciously and covered her cleavage with the stack of books she was holding.

"Do you work here?" I asked with a slightly embarrassed smile of my own.

"No. I just came to look for some materials for a paper I am preparing for the university. If you want to find English articles, the best thing to do is to go over to the Post. They will be glad to help you."

"Where is their office? As you can see, I'm not from around here and I don't really know the city yet."

"If you will wait a few minutes, I can take you there. It is on my way home, in the middle of the old city, Bella Ciudad Baja. I just need to pay the cashier. It won't take long."

"Gracias. That would be wonderful. I'll wait for you there," I replied.

She smiled at me and headed toward the counter where the malicious manager was still playing around with her stack of newspapers.

I could not stop staring at my young savior and admiring her unbelievable figure. I'll admit, I was very excited. That attractive young woman with her bright smile and wonderful green eyes had my blood boiling.

A few minutes later, we were walking together through the long library corridor. Even with the black high-heeled shoes she was wearing, her pace was fast enough to match my large strides.

I inhaled the sweet smell of her hair and noticed her shy smile. She absolutely intrigued me.

"Where are you from?" she asked without turning her head toward me.

"Los Angeles," I answered.

She looked at me and said, "So I will ask you the same thing as the border police asked you. Are you here for business or for pleasure?"

"Business," I replied. "I was invited to do a job. Unfortunately, I do not think I will have a lot of time for pleasure."

She lowered her eyes and said, "Excuse me, but I am curious. I hope it is not rude to ask what kind of job it is—something interesting?"

"No, it's not rude at all, and yes, I think the job is interesting. At least if you find security and protection to be an interesting profession."

"I think it is very interesting," she said with enthusiasm. "There was even a time when I wanted to join the police. There are not a lot of people I know who can truly say they find interest in their work, and I think that police work is a field with a lot of challenges. After I finish school, I might join the police academy."

"What do you study?"

"English literature, I like it very much, but when I graduate, I will probably have to be a high school teacher. I think it would be better to be a detective."

"You would have to be a very brave woman to even consider such a career path."

"I don't know if I'm brave, but I'm definitely not a coward." She suddenly stopped and pointed to a bench. "Wait for me here while I get my car. I hope it will not take long, OK?"

"Sure, and thank you, again."

She turned around. I remained standing, giving myself another chance to marvel at her beautiful figure. 'What a nice birthday present,' I thought to myself.

If it weren't for Meeka, I would have made every effort to get closer—a lot closer—to this smiling angel. However, there was Meeka, and though she was now many miles away in Los Angeles preparing to return to Israel, I could not forget her and did not want to act as a carefree bachelor.

In our two months together, something was built—a connection of some sort that was unique and worth preserving. I did not want to risk it, even from afar, not even for a little adventure with a young, green-eyed beauty.

I sat down on the bench and waited. The thought of Meeka gave me a pleasant sensation of warmth and tranquility. I was somewhat annoyed for allowing myself to get so light-headed in the presence of the Mexican student. My phone's vibration abruptly brought me back to reality. It was Jody.

"I spoke with the people from Guardian. They'll wait for you to come back."

"Great. What else?"

"That's it. Is everything all right with you?"

"Yes, so far, so good, I've got to go—I'll talk to you later. Bye."

The young lady who had volunteered to take me to the Post newspaper had just driven up in her white Peugeot. As I walked toward her car, I felt that pleasant excitement taking over my body. All my attempts to keep Meeka in mind failed. The presence of such rare beauty was overwhelming.

"Shall we go?" she asked.

"Sure, why not?" I answered, hiding my inner turmoil the best that my training and experience had taught me.

It was then that I realized I didn't even know her name.

"Elisa Rosario Hernandez," she answered quickly while

quite skillfully navigating her car into the traffic on the busy city street. "Call me 'Elisa' or 'Lisa,' whichever you prefer. And what's your name?"

"Ethan, Ethan Eshed."

She looked at me with surprise.

"Eshed? I've never heard that last name before. What kind of a name is that? It is not an American name, is it?"

"You're right, it's not. It's an Israeli name. I was born in Israel, but I have lived and worked in the U.S. for the last eight years. Do you know much about Israel?"

"I don't know a lot about it. Just general stuff: Middle East, Jesus, Holy Land, Nazareth, Jerusalem and that there is a war going on all the time. That's it, more or less. Not a lot, is it?"

She maneuvered her car swiftly and confidently through the dense traffic dominated by a large fleet of taxis driven with no regard to safe and considerate driving practices.

"Here," she said suddenly, pointing to a tall building right on the corner. "This is the Post building. I'll just pull over here."

If it were up to me, I would have stayed in her car forever. My brain raced to find a way to keep in touch with her. "I would love to thank you for your help. Can I invite you to dinner, or..."

"There is no need really," she answered quickly as she turned off the engine. 'That's a good sign; at least she is not in a hurry to run away from me,' I thought to myself.

"I was glad to help someone who doesn't speak the language, and I gave him a lift, that's all."

"Nevertheless, I want to thank you," I found myself insisting like a 16-year-old in love. "It doesn't have to be dinner, but at least a drink, no commitment—just to show my gratitude."

She shrugged.

"It's not that I'm trying to avoid you, but I am very busy with school. I have to turn in this paper, and I work in the evenings. So I really don't know. You know what? Give me your hotel phone number and I will call you, but you really don't have to…"

I was not willing to give up. "I do have to, and I want to very much," I said quickly. "I am staying at El Presidente, room 1021. I don't know the phone number there, but it's easy to find. Ask for Ethan Eshed."

The girl and her green eyes smiled at me.

"Room 1021, El Presidente, Ethan Eshed. I will remember."

"Will you call?" I asked getting out of the car. "I will be waiting for your phone call."

A split second later, she was gone. My years of training did not fail me. I got her license plate number: 307-HET.

5.

Disappointment awaited me at the Post. I was told that public viewing is only allowed in the morning hours. I tried to plead, but it did not help. They were not willing to make an exception. The director of the Public Relations department, a heavy-set woman wearing a miniskirt which revealed way too much flesh turned me down with an uncompromising smile.

"I am very sorry, Sir. You will have to return tomorrow morning. We will be glad to assist you then."

For the second time within hours, that intolerable feeling of helplessness arose. I realized that I was almost completely dependent upon others. That was an unbearable situation in my line of work.

It was not only my lack of detailed information on the two people with whom I was getting involved, Valencia and Cortez, but my biggest frustration was that I had to rely on Cortez's willingness to cooperate with me and update me, truthfully, on everything that had happened. It also looked as if I would need his operational assistance. The fear that he might try to set me up for failure was real.

I was sure that he would not do so in a way that could

be traced back to him. However, it was clear that I had been called in to succeed where he had failed. My success would just highlight his failure. I was sure Cortez was not a person who would allow anyone to expose his weaknesses. He would never forgive me if that were the outcome. He definitely would not hand me the rope that would hang him. Although in Mexico, this might turn into the reality.

Concerned and deflated, I returned to my hotel room. It had been cleaned and the bar, restocked.

In all the cases I have taken as a private investigator, intricate and uncomplicated alike, I always insisted on handpicking the teams who would get the job done. They had to be people I trusted and knew were the best for the specific task at hand. That was the only way I was confident that things would be done right and that full and accurate information could be accessed. The chance of having to rely on personnel loyal to Cortez was unappealing, and that was an understatement.

I lay on the bed gathering my thoughts, trying to ignore my image in the mirror on the ceiling. I was trying to analyze what seemed to be a very complex relationship between Valencia and his son-in-law.

On the one hand, the hierarchy was clear and visible. There was no doubt that Valencia was the almighty and uncontested boss. During our meeting earlier, Cortez had made deliberate respectful gestures toward his father-in-law, leaving all decision making to him. On the other hand, I could not help noticing that in spite of Cortez's façade of subservience, he might be the one who had the power of execution in all of Valencia's matters. Not just in this specific case, but with other issues as well, this 'wimp' might be a very powerful man with absolute authority in Valencia's entourage. It could even be that to some degree, Cortez had a massive behind-the-scenes influence on Valencia himself.

It was crucial for me to determine how much Valencia trusted Cortez, and even more so, the level of influence and source of power that Cortez had over Valencia.

Another thing I had to figure out was how aware Valencia was of all of the details in this case. I had a feeling that even though he wanted it to appear that he did not care about the small details, this was not true.

I couldn't resist toying with the idea that it was actually Jorge Cortez, the person in charge of the operation to find the kidnappers, the son-in-law and confidante behind the abduction. It was like a Hollywood movie for Vice President Cortez to be the bad guy in this story. The half hour I spent with him earlier was more than enough time for me to formulate an opinion on his personality: repulsive. He projected zero credibility. I did not have any facts to back my feelings, but I had a sense that Valencia shared my opinion of Cortez. That may indeed be the reason why I was here.

The newspaper clippings could have given answers, or at least clues to these questions. Maybe over dinner with Cortez, which was supposed to happen in about an hour and a half, I would be able to justify some of my intuitions.

There was also the time constraint that did not allow for any real strategic planning. In the four days since the kidnapping, two phone conversations had already taken place and the third one that was scheduled for tomorrow night would probably deal with finalizing the ransom and exchange. There was not enough time, and I knew that action without planning could lead to a disaster. In this context, that could mean the life of a little girl.

As I got off the bed to get ready for my meeting with Cortez, I made two decisions: I needed my own people here regardless of whether Cortez liked it or not, and I had to delay things somewhat, at least until Rob arrived.

Thinking of making decisions under pressure made me remember my morning conversation with Jeanne. My decision to have Jeanne and Alan serve the court subpoena to the video distributor rather than have them wait for me to do it was contrary to a rule I had set for myself ever since I had begun working as a private investigator.

I had always insisted on being there when a case closed. It was not because I thought I was the only one who could do it, or that I did not trust my people. I believed that my clients hired me because they believed in me and my qualifications. They wanted to know that I was personally performing the work for which they were paying.

This time there was no alternative. Even in the most optimistic scenario, I could not see this case in Mexico wrapping up in a couple of days. I would not be flying to the Netherlands. I had to entrust Jeanne and Alan with the serving of the subpoena, and hope for the best.

At the same time, I was thinking about Lisa, and that made my heart beat at a faster-than-normal rate. In my 44 years, especially after my divorce from Dianne, I had met many women. Most of them were very pretty, not many were beautiful. Lisa was truly beautiful.

Since Lisa initiated the contact between us in the library, I started to think that our coincidental meeting was not coincidental at all. Maybe somebody did his homework and knew about my tastes, what type of woman would attract me, and tried to investigate the investigator. Accidentally meeting the most beautiful woman in the world only happens in James Bond movies.

Ignoring the alarm bells ringing in my head, I smiled to myself. Her image—face, eyes and most of all, that smile filled my mind. I quelled my previous worries, questions and concerns. She was really wonderful, and since she had not given me any reason to suspect her intentions were anything but sincere, I set aside my paranoia and indulged in the pleasant sensation that filled me whenever I saw her in my mind.

I realized that what really excited me about her, apart from her physicality, was an immediate sense of familiarity and closeness that made me feel as if we had been together forever.

Trying to set aside my thoughts of Lisa, I found myself sitting on the edge of the bed calling Meeka.

"Hi, Meeka," I said. "How are you doing?"

"I'm OK. Fine." Her voice was cold and restrained. "Nothing special. How are you?"

I lay on the bed with the phone pressed tightly to my ear. "I just got in. I have an amazing hotel suite with a half-acre bed. You would love it. It's a pity that you're not here with me."

She was silent.

Hurt, I continued my dry, factual report.

"I am tying to figure out what I need to do with this case. I think it will take at least a week, maybe even more."

There was no response.

"I miss you," I said without thinking twice. "It would have been so nice to be here together. They say there are wonderful things to see around here, not that I have had the chance to see anything yet."

Finally, she answered.

"You know that's impossible. I still don't know how I will manage to do everything by the time I have to leave. I haven't finished shopping for all the gifts I have to bring, and in two days, I'm out of here."

"I will miss you, Meeka"

Again, she was silent. I waited for what seemed to be an eternity.

"Did you hear what I said?"

"I heard you."

"And you have nothing to say?"

I heard her sigh, "What do you want me to say? Don't you know that I will miss you even more? You think that it's easy for me now, but I'm trying…"

"What? What are you trying?" I teased her.

There was a pause, and then she spoke in her rational, balanced, 'I've thought of everything' voice,

"I am trying to be realistic, and I am aware that it sounds cold, but I am not going to play the missing game with you when I am on one side of the globe and you are on the other."

"That can change," I said. "It's no longer a big deal to take a plane and be wherever you want within hours. I do it every time I miss my daughter."

"Ethan, what do you want? You know I love you, and I wish we could be together forever and ever, but I am not built for a long-distance relationship. For me, 'what is close to the eye is close to the heart.' I am not willing to miss someone in California while living in Israel. You know that. I told you. We talked about it."

"And you are willing to give up so easily on what we had going for these two months?"

She was silent.

Beaten, I muttered, "It is so hard for me to understand you."

"What's so hard to understand? There is only one possible solution. Come back. If you love me as much as you say you do, come with me. Your daughter is there. You will regret till your last days that you were not there to see her grow up from a little girl into a woman. Believe me that whatever it is you are doing here, you can do there."

"I don't think I can. Actually, I'm sure I can't."

6.

I preferred spending the hour I had left before my early dinner with Jorge Cortez at the hotel bar. My last conversation with Meeka left me with a very sour taste in my mouth that only alcohol would remove.

I guess it was out of habit that I sat down in the one seat that enabled me to see everything that was going on around me. Looking through the big lobby windows, I watched rain crowding out the beautiful weather that had welcomed me that day. Now the weather reflected my feelings exactly. I was so upset earlier that I didn't even notice that Meeka hadn't remembered that today was my birthday. Realizing she forgot made the insult I was feeling even worse.

I was surprised at how she viewed the future of our relationship. I had heard it before—no matter how much she loved me, she had to go, she did not believe in a long-distance relationship, and so on. However, the feelings that we had developed for each other in just two short months were precious to me beyond anything I had experienced since my divorce.

For the first time in many years, I had met a woman

with whom I thought I could share my life. I loved her looks, her relaxed way of living, her pragmatic point of view, her analytic thinking, her cold and rational observations, and most of all, the intimacy that swept me away to emotional places I thought had ceased to exist in me.

As much as I hated to admit it, and hated even more to hear Meeka say over and over again, her argument made a lot of sense. 'I have no intention of sitting at home even for one evening, putting my life on hold for you while I might be missing out on something real that makes sense.'

"What good would it do?" she would ask repeatedly, in that same cold and rational tone that instinctively took over whenever she felt pressured. I guessed it was learned in law school, or maybe one needed to possess that skill to be accepted there in the first place. 'It totally doesn't make sense. I don't want to have the burden of loyalty around my neck when at the end of the day you are not there. I do not want to lie to you and I do not need the constant conscience check that comes with it.'

"Good evening, Sir. Can I offer you a drink?"

The bartender's question shocked me back to the reality of Mexico City and the reason I was here.

"Whisky on the rocks, please."

"Right away, Sir," replied the bartender. I noticed he was tall with a thin, neatly groomed mustache. His English had an accent I couldn't place. He had probably lived in many different countries and had developed a hybrid kind of accent.

I gazed at a young couple sitting on the other end of the bar, kissing and holding each other passionately. In the smoke-filled darkness it was difficult to see details, but their slowly moving silhouettes made a feeling of envy creep up my spine.

This whole day seemed to be about new feelings and sensations, because this one also caught me by surprise.

I was used to being by myself as a policeman, and then as a private investigator. Yet, I'd never remembered feeling lonely. Being a 'Lone Ranger,' a man operating alone with no dependence on or ties to his social surroundings, never bothered me. On the contrary, I learned to like and appreciate the advantages of anonymity both on a personal and professional level.

I loved the days, sometimes weeks, when I was alone in a foreign city or country, totally involved in whatever case I had taken on. I was never bored and never felt a need for companionship. I was always able to find a woman that would pleasure me in those not-too-many free hours my ever-busy schedule allowed, and I'd neither needed nor asked for more.

So what was it that made me envious of that anonymous couple making out at the bar? Maybe it was a reaction to my conversation with Meeka. Maybe it was something deeper. Maybe I was reaching an age at which you develop a need for stability in a relationship and a home.

These last few weeks with her had me thinking quite a lot about it. After so many years of living a carefree existence, maybe it was time to grow up, as my parents said, meaning it was time to get married.

In my mind, establishing some kind of permanent relationship with Meeka was a done deal. However, the price she put on it was impossible for me to pay.

Nobody in Israel was waiting for me with open arms, at least not professionally. Many media people held me responsible for the fall of their beloved Aviram Melamedovitch. Years after the story the media headlined as "The Case of the Officer and his Mama" that led to Rob's retirement, Mr. Melamedovitch was arrested in Nice, France. The French police found four million counterfeit Euro notes in his hotel suite. The tip to the French authorities was made by a source with whom I was working at the time. I never took credit for the arrest, but the media somehow sensed I was involved and did not leave me alone on this issue.

"Here is your drink *Señor*. Will you be paying cash or are you a hotel guest, Sir?"

"I'll sign. I'm a hotel guest," I said. It was still raining outside and people were running to find shelter, but the bar was still almost empty. Even the couple who was there earlier had left the bar, probably to their room to finish what they'd started.

I took a large sip from my drink. I felt a pleasant heat wave taking over. I reached for a little bowl and fished out a pair of olives.

From the other side of the counter, the barman said, "I have been living in Mexico for seven years now and I still can not get used to this crazy weather; it surprises me every time. It starts with a beautiful morning, hot and sunny, and then, suddenly it rains. It is definitely not normal."

I smiled at him. "Where are you from?" I asked, taking out another olive.

"I am from Palestine," he said laying out a dozen beer glasses on a tray in a geometrical order. He looked at me with a smile. "Have you heard of Palestine? Do you know where it is?"

I nodded with an expression of indifference. I did not introduce myself as an Israeli, even though that is what I consider myself to be in spite of my many years in Los Angeles. It was better to maintain the American-tourist image. It seemed much safer under the circumstances.

"A lot of action in your neck of the woods," I answered and attended to my drink. His name tag read 'Muhammad Abbas.' I memorized his name. You never know.

He smiled, exposing two lines of snowy-white teeth.

"Too much action, Sir. I lived in a city called Gaza. I don't know if you've heard the name. It's in the north of the Sinai Desert by the Mediterranean Sea. If you want to live a normal life, it's not the place to be. You can't live there like a decent human being. So one day, I just left. I wandered for a few years from country to country: Germany, Canada, the U.S., and I ended up here, in Mexico. I like a quiet life, simple. I have a house here, a job, food and friends—everything a man needs to live a normal life. The only anomaly here is the weather."

I smiled, following his skilled and graceful hand motions as he polished the beer mugs. I appreciated professionalism in all occupations, and it seemed as though he definitely was a master at his. However, it was not my intention to enter into a conversation.

I made a habit of letting my colleagues in the *Mossad*, the Israeli Intelligence Bureau, know about any Palestinian person I meet who might be an asset to them. I try to learn as much as I can about the person and his motivations. Many of those who escaped the daily horror of life in the areas captured by the Israeli Army (occupied territories) during the 1967 war are willing to assist the Israelis in return for benefits for themselves or their relatives left behind. I was sure that this person had a lot to offer, however, this time around, I was way too busy as it was.

"Maybe you can tell me how to get to Barbarosa Restaurant?" I asked as I emptied my glass. "Is it far away or can I walk there?"

He put a glass down.

"It is not very far away. You exit the hotel and take a

left, at the first street, go left again. After you pass all the embassies, you make a final left."

"But," he hesitated and stared at me with his big, dark eyes, "I would not recommend walking there. After sunset in Mexico City is not a pleasant time to be out walking. There are all types out there, you know. I would advise you to take a taxi. It's much safer."

7.

Jorge Cortez was not just an ideal host. It turned out that he was a seasoned professional, validating the saying, "Don't judge a book by its cover."

After two and a half hours face to face in one of the small private booths of Barbarosa, savoring each bite of an exquisite meal, I admired the show he arranged for me, but realized that I could not afford to underestimate the man behind it.

The large, yet intimately lit space of the restaurant with its many small tables and row of private booths was a perfect stage for Cortez to play the part of the concerned host wanting to please his guest. He went out of his way to impress me. He tried to give me the feeling he was willing to not only serve me delicious food but also chew it for me if that is what I desired.

He performed masterfully as an alert and attentive conversationalist as well. He maneuvered between informative items and things that were 'for my ears only,' from sentimental personal memories to scandalous gossip. My somewhat aloof and formal attitude did not stop him from acting like I was a long-lost friend he hadn't seen in ages.

Without a doubt, he was a professional. His knowledge of issues of security and protection was remarkable. He answered all of my questions and more.

"I imagine you are surprised that I am willing to cooperate without any reservations," he noted, smiling while I was writing everything he said in my little notebook.

"In your position, I would be suspicious as well, but you've got to believe that in this case there is no room for ego. It is not important who brings Carmen home, the important thing is that she will return home unharmed. The rest is insignificant."

I did not respond to that last statement of his.

"Did you investigate the possibility that business or personal rivals of Mr. Valencia are behind this for the sole purpose of harming him and not just for the money? Maybe someone wanted to create a personal crisis which would distract him so that he could be taken advantage of in some business dealing?"

Cortez laughed. He gently pushed his plate forward and took a pack of cigarettes out of his pocket.

"Of course we've thought about it, Mr. Eshed. We know our work, even though at this time, we do not have a lot of results to show for it."

Again, I did not respond. His smile faded.

"Wisdom was not given solely to the Israelis. I know you have a lot of police and military experience, but we are not amateurs. We know what we are supposed to do."

He lit his cigarette and smoked silently for a while. His eyes were fixed on a distant spot behind me. I read his message clearly. What he wanted to convey was: 'We have done our homework and we know everything there is to know about you.' I wondered what that knowledge included beyond my military and police background.

After a few more seconds, he was back in control of himself.

He looked at me directly and said, "As you probably know by now, Mr. Valencia is involved in many different types of business, and as we say here in Mexico, 'If you tell me how many enemies you have, I will tell you how successful you are.' I can easily name 10 people who would like to hurt him or take revenge for some personal or business affair. The short list includes some of the most well-known and influential politicians in Mexico. We haven't even started counting his rivals from other countries or..."

"Everyone has enemies and rivals," I interrupted, "but is there anyone who Mr. Valencia has ever seriously insulted? Something that would make a man risk everything—his reputation, his money and even his life in order to take revenge on Mr. Valencia?"

"Let's take Alfonso Ortega as an example," said Cortez quickly. "Between Ortega and Mr. Valencia, there is a rivalry that goes back many years. It is very bitter and concerns business mostly, but there are also personal complications. The two are distant relatives."

Cortez blew three rings of cigarette smoke while his eyes remained affixed upon that same spot behind me.

"There was this story...about 10 years ago...Ortega accused Mr. Valencia of trying to steal his mistress. I don't know if its true, but you know, 'There is no smoke without a fire.' You can say a lot about Mr. Valencia, but a woman hater he is not. Anyway, that is old news. However, a few months back, the rivalry resurfaced because of the "Panorama" story. Do you know what that is all about?"

I was not ready for that question. My heart skipped a beat. I hated my hasty decision to get involved in this case without the proper preparations and the vital background information I so desperately needed at this exact moment.

With great effort, I was able to keep a straight face and answer, "I know, but I think it would be best if I heard it from you because you, of course, have the most complete and accurate details."

Cortez's eyes, which had been momentarily focused on my face, moved again to the same place that for some reason had attracted him throughout the evening. Suddenly, he smiled.

"With your permission," he said, while standing up, "I spotted two friends of mine who I have not seen for a long time. If you will forgive me, I will go and say hi."

He got out of the booth, and a few seconds later, he was in a group hug with two young women: a tall, well-built blonde and an anorexic-looking girl with short hair.

I was about to bite into an incredibly tempting piece of steak when I heard Cortez's voice. "Mr. Eshed, I would like to introduce you to two very good friends of mine. Mia, this is Mr. Eshed, my longtime friend from Los Angeles."

I stood up and mumbled, "It's my pleasure," to the young blonde who was about to burst out of her skin-tight miniskirt at any second. She smiled, undressing me with her eyes.

"And this is Luna," continued Cortez. "She used to work for me, but now she manages her own very successful manpower company. Luna, this is Mr. Eshed."

We shook hands. She had light-blue eyes and wore a black, mannish suit.

"Hi," she said, smiling. "I am very happy to meet you."

Cortez stood by the girls like a proud father of the bride. Suddenly he put his arm around my shoulders and whispered in my ear.

"Ethan, look, I hope this is OK with you, I would like to invite these girls to join us, if you don't mind, of course."

I took a step back, releasing myself from his embrace and whispered back to him, "Maybe later. We have business to finish and time is not on our side as you know."

"No, no, you are absolutely right. It is better that we continue, of course."

Cortez turned to the girls, hugged them both and said something in Spanish. The girls waved to me and went back to their table at the other end of the restaurant.

"I hope you are not angry with me," said Cortez as he sat back at the table. "It's just two beautiful girls. Well, it could be nice."

"Absolutely," I replied, "but as we say, business before pleasure."

"I understand."

I admit that at first I believed that meeting the two women in the restaurant was by chance, and I felt a little guilty for ruining it for him, but then he leaned over and said in a secretive whisper, "I don't think they will object to joining us later for a little party after we finish our business. Did you see how the blonde was staring at you?"

All that shouldn't have surprised me. I was fairly used to my hosts trying to make my stay enjoyable, and that often included offers of this nature.

In this particular case, it was an offer I could refuse with no hesitation. The idea of 'partying' with Cortez sounded disgusting. I also knew that every weakness I allowed Cortez to exploit would be played against me at some point. I am sure that while doing his research, he learned of my affection for young, beautiful women.

However, one point he probably missed was that *I* decide whom I consider beautiful and with whom I party.

"I'm not in the mood for a party tonight. What I need is a good night's sleep. Tomorrow is a crucial day and I need to be at my best. Thanks anyway."

"No need to thank me," he answered. "It is my pleasure. You decide what is best for you. I just want you to know that it is an open invitation whenever you like. I personally believe that if the body is free of toxins and stress, the mind works better. We have a saying…"

At this point, I tuned out.

Finally, we got back to talking about Carmen. Cortez recapped the timeline of the ambush and kidnapping. He also gave me the names of the driver and bodyguard. He described what he called their "diversionary tactic" to get anyone who might ask questions off their backs, especially the police. They leaked to one of the gossip columnists that Carmen had a "mysterious illness." It worked; the tabloids ate it up.

"Mr. Valencia insisted this morning that we not involve the police in the case. I know that it would make my presence here redundant, but if it saves the girl, why not do it?"

Cortez stopped me with a sharp gesture.

"Forget it. I have known him for a long time. If he decided he does not want the police in on this, there is no chance that he will go back on his word. He has had a very bad experience with the police in this type of situation and…"

I looked at him, puzzled.

Cortez explained, "When his niece Mariana was kidnapped, we called the police. An officer, Rodrigo Gonzales, headed the police team. It is now clear that if it had not been for him, Mariana would still be alive today.

As I have hopefully proven to you, I know something about investigations. From my point of view, Gonzales made all the mistakes in the book. I could have forgiven him if he was an idiot, but he is a good officer, and that leads me to only one possible conclusion: Someone paid him to mess this one up. This is why Mr. Valencia would never contact the police to help save Carmen."

8.

Suddenly, I noticed a pair of green eyes gazing at me from outside the booth. It was a young girl with her hair neatly pulled back, wearing a white shirt and a black skirt like the rest of the restaurant employees. 'Oh my god!' I exclaimed to myself as I recognized Lisa, holding a huge tray full of delightful-looking dishes.

I waved my hand at her, thinking how she had filled my imagination for the entire afternoon. She smiled shyly.

"I see you really do not require my help in meeting beautiful women," said Cortez from the other side of the table. I saw that he was staring at Lisa with a troubled look. I smiled at him. I did not intend for Cortez to notice that all my attention was actually focused on making contact with Lisa.

"I usually work alone," I said in a humble voice. "Sometimes I'm successful and sometimes, so-so. You know how it goes."

I was looking at Cortez, but thinking of Lisa. I was growing very affectionate toward her, and given this second chance, I was determined to make the most of it.

"Please excuse me. I will be right back," said my host.

"Should we order dessert? They have the best crème brûlée I have ever tasted. I highly recommend it."

"As you like," I answered calmly, waiting for him to disappear so that I could look for Lisa. I closed my eyes and counted to 10. Then I opened my eyes and turned my head. She was standing right in front of me, smiling.

"I came to say hi," she said.

I stood up, taking in every inch of her from head to toe. With her high-heeled shoes and the way she was wearing her hair, she looked younger and even prettier than I had remembered.

"Hi. I was afraid I would not see you again," I said taking her hand. Even if I wanted to—and I didn't—I could not hide my joy.

Her little hand got lost in mine. The warmth of that contact revealed a growing fondness between us.

"Are you enjoying yourself here?" she asked, in no hurry to release her hand from mine.

"Yes, very much," I answered. "I guess you work here."

She pulled her hand away gently; her eyes locked with mine and penetrated me. "Someone has to pay for my tuition." She said, as her eyes started to well up. "I am not from a wealthy family. I have no choice. I need to take care of myself."

"I am very sorry we are not at your table. I would have made sure you got a good tip."

She laughed. "You are very kind. Thank you."

I noticed Cortez as he came out of the restroom.

"When do you finish here?" I asked quickly. "This time I am not giving up so easily."

She smiled sadly.

"It will be late, and I have to wake up early tomorrow. I'm sorry."

I changed my tactics.

"Too bad," I said as though with regret. "It is your loss. I have a business proposition for you—nothing complicated and it pays well."

I saw her interest peak.

"It will not take a lot of your time and you will be paid well. Just a second ago you told me you needed to pay for your own education. This is your chance."

I didn't lie to her. Earlier at the Post, I regretted not offering her a job as an assistant helping me with the research. Instead of me running around town looking for information in English, she could find articles about Valencia, Cortez, their rivals and companies, as well as any other information I might need. She could read through the three Spanish newspapers and summarize them for me in English. It would be an optimal arrangement for me, and a profitable one for her. It was an offer that would be hard for her to reject.

"I need you for two or three days, not more. You will need to do what I tried to do unsuccessfully today at the library."

"Do you really want to offer me a job or are you just looking for an excuse to see me?"

"I am really offering you a job, but that doesn't mean that I don't want to see you. I would love to get to know you a little better. When should I pick you up?"

She was still hesitant.

"We usually close at 11, and it takes another half hour to clean the place. I can only meet for 30 minutes; I really have to wake up very early tomorrow."

"I'll wait for you outside at 11:30 p.m."

"OK," she sighed. "But only for half an hour."

She turned around. Hurrying toward the kitchen, she greeted Cortez as she passed him. When he sat back down, he had a wide, sleazy grin on his face.

"I admire your taste. When did you have time to meet Alice…no, Lisa? That's her name, right?"

I had no intention of voluntarily giving away information.

"She is a good girl," he continued. "To tell the truth, I tried to seduce her a few times, but was never successful. She refused me every time. She's a really good girl. Anyway, I ordered dessert. I hope you like it."

"Thanks," I said. "While we're waiting, I have a few more questions."

Cortez's face wore a serious expression.

"This is what we are here for. I hope you are not suggesting that I am trying to avoid the issue. I am just very fond of mixing business with pleasure, that's all."

"I need to know a little more about Mariana's kidnapping, and if you think there might be any connection between the two cases?"

Cortez hesitated for a few seconds. Just as he began to answer, our waitress, who looked like a younger version of the actress Emma Thompson, appeared with a gold-plated tray. "Your crème brûlée, enjoy!" she announced enthusiastically.

His face lit up. He looked at the two copper bowls.

"This looks superb," he said lustily. "If there is something I can not resist, it is crème brûlée!"

He attacked his serving ferociously, encouraging me to do the same.

"I imagine that you are already full, but you've got to try this."

I looked at him eating. His eyes shut with pleasure, mumbling in Spanish, "¡Que rico! ¡Que rico! ¡Que rico!"

Actually, it really was the best crème brûlée I had ever tasted. No more business was discussed that evening.

9.

I was delayed more than I expected. I made a phone call to Jody instructing her to rush two teams here: Gila and Ricardo, and Alejandro and Miguel. I took another phone call from Rob, notifying me of his departure to Mexico City. Then I changed from my dress clothes into my preferred attire: a black T-shirt and jeans. This caused me to arrive back at Barbarosa at 11:34 p.m. Lisa was waiting for me outside. Dressed in tight jeans and an open jean jacket that covered a white tank top, she looked stunning.

"I thought something happened to you. I was starting to get worried!"

I smiled. It pleased me to hear that she was worried, even though we barely knew each other. Her attempt to look her best for our late-night meeting after a busy shift at work showed an intention that made me hopeful.

"Don't worry," I said. "The worst that could happen would be for me to lose my way, but I'm pretty good with directions." We were standing very close and the smell of her perfume was enticing.

"Mexico City can be very confusing. It looks so quiet and lovely, but if you do not know your way around, you might find yourself in a dangerous situation. Many tourists out for an evening stroll have been attacked, mugged and even murdered."

"Well, I'm here, safe and sound. I just had some business to take care of. Do you know a nice place in the area where we can sit and talk?"

She thought for a few seconds and said, "Yes, there is a small place just around the corner. Let's go."

She reached for my hand and pulled me after her.

"Hey! What's the rush?" I asked enjoying the warmth of her hand.

Avenida de La Reforma was very busy at this time of night. Locals and tourists filled the coffee shops and clubs in the district. The rain had stopped a few hours ago and people were out in the streets enjoying the warm evening air.

We passed the Carousel nightclub. Its deafening music could be heard even out here on the street. We turned left onto a side street.

"Here we are. We can sit quietly and talk here." She pointed to a wide-open door.

Her openness and warmth, as well as the fact that we still held hands tightly, made me want to skip the business part and go straight to the pleasure. Meeka seemed to be part of some parallel universe, and I had no intention of leaving this one. I was enjoying myself way too much.

As we entered the restaurant, we were surrounded by the smell of incense and the sound of Indian music. We sat on a large sofa at the far end of the room.

"I need something to drink," she said as she signaled to the girl behind the bar. "The work at the restaurant really makes me thirsty."

She ordered iced tea and I had my usual whisky on the rocks. A couple walked by looking for an empty seat.

Lisa quickly explained, "Sorry, these seats are taken. We are expecting some friends. They are on their way."

Leaning closely toward me, she said, "We don't want company now, do we?"

It was as if she had read my mind. I decided to get the business part out of the way quickly.

I briefly told her what I needed.

"I'll pay you 100 dollars a day. If it's not enough, then tell me and I will see what I can do."

"Are you crazy? It's way too much. I can't accept so much. This is a two-week salary for just one day of work. Ethan, this is Mexico. I'll tell you what. I will do the job because it sounds very interesting and not too hard. When I finish, and if you are pleased, we can decide on how much you'll pay. Deal?"

"Yeah, sure. I'm not going to argue, but you have to agree that you are working for me and it's my decision how much to pay. Now, deal?"

"OK. Deal! So tell me, how do you know Cortez, and why are he and his boss so important to you that you need to know everything that has been written about them in the newspapers?"

"We are supposed to do something together. You could call it business. I believe you know him?"

She laughed and looked at her glass.

"This is delicious. You can't imagine how tired you get waiting tables for five hours."

Her expression turned serious.

"I don't know what it is between you two, but I suggest that you be careful with him—very careful."

At that moment all I wanted was to hug her. I was fascinated by her ingenuousness.

"Why do you think I should be careful? What do you know about him?"

"I know what everybody knows from the media, and I know from personal experience that he is a ruthless womanizer. I saw how he tried to force his two sluts on you. Watching you turn them down and disappoint Cortez pleased me. You're quite a man to refuse that kind of free desert."

"Well, had I accepted his offer, we wouldn't be sitting here right now, would we?"

She blushed and I continued.

"I can see that you really don't like him. Did he…"

"He tried to seduce me a few times. Many of the girls in the restaurant have been with him. He is very rich and spends his money freely, but he's a creep. I hate it when men think that they can get anything with their money. I am not for sale."

She hesitated for a second.

"Maybe it is not wise for me to talk about him this way since you two are partners."

"It's all right. I am not part of his fan club either. That is the reason I need to know all there is to know about him. Look," I said as I took her hand in mine, "I am working for someone and part of the bargain is cooperating with him. Unfortunately, thinking of him reminds me of the maxim, 'Never turn your back on a rattlesnake.'"

She laughed and looked down at our hands with our fingers tightly interwoven.

"To be honest with you," she said after a few seconds, "I am a little disappointed."

I looked at her, puzzled.

"I thought that you were interested in me, but it seems that all you want is for me to work for you."

I couldn't figure out if she was kidding or not. Her expression was very serious, yet she still sat temptingly close with her hand in mine.

Trying to get some clarity, I asked, "Do you really want our relationship to be more than business?"

"I don't know you at all," she said, tightening her grip on my hand. "All I know is your name and that I feel good when I am with you. How long are you planning to stay in Mexico City?"

"It is not clear yet—maybe a week, maybe more. It depends on how things turn out."

We talked for what seemed like an eternity. It felt like we had known each other forever. People came and went. Even our waitress finished her shift and a new one started hers.

She was 25 years old. She described her family as an average conservative Mexican family. Her father worked as a carpenter while her ailing mother was a housewife. Two married brothers and a sister who left for Los Angeles three years ago completed the family portrait.

According to Lisa, her sister had to leave to escape her father's stranglehold.

"He is impossible," she said as she played with my fingers. "He is stuck somewhere in the Middle Ages and can't accept that we are living in a modern society. I think that if he saw me in a bar holding hands with a man who might be married..."

"Divorced. I have a 10-year-old daughter, Natalie. I am 44 and I am a private investigator," I said, looking at her directly and smiling. "Do you know how happy I am that I met you? I don't think you know how special you are."

If I had to decide between Lisa and Meeka, at this moment it was Lisa by a landslide. She was warm and open, trusting and enthusiastic. She had captured my heart.

She looked at me deeply, and then smiled.

"I really don't know what's going to happen and where this road leads. Chances are that in a week or two, our paths will part. I don't care. Whatever will be will be. I feel so good now that I don't want to think about the future."

I gently pulled her toward me. Slowly our lips met. Her breasts pressed against my chest as she wrapped her arms around me. It was as if we were melting together in pure happiness.

10.

It was around 2 a.m. when I got back to the hotel. I was way too excited to go to sleep and had to take two cold showers to chill my burning body. I turned on my laptop and started to surf the Internet.

At 5 a.m., I sent two e-mails to Jody and one to Gila, who would head up the team arriving to assist me in this assignment. I detailed each of their duties and what I expected from them.

One team would observe the Valencia mansion and list everyone entering or leaving, while the other team would look for information about all the visitors. I believed this strategy would allow us to compile some very useful data that could help us later.

Between showers and e-mails, I devised my plan for this case.

The most important thing was to buy as much time as possible to allow the teams to collect information and start a methodological investigation. Luck was on our side since tomorrow was a national holiday. The banks were working holiday hours and most places of business were closed. It would be very reasonable for Valencia to request a few more days with the excuse that the holiday would prevent him from putting together the money that had been requested. I also had a plan for the next phone conversation with the kidnappers. It was risky, but I knew that this was the only way we could lure them from their hideout. Finally, I fell asleep.

I woke up with a huge headache. I tried to relieve the pain by thinking of Lisa and the events of last night. It helped a little. However, I still felt pretty lousy while I was driving with Rob from our meeting with Valencia at the mansion. They all accepted my plan to stall the kidnappers, and we did a little bit of role-play to prepare for the phone call that evening.

To avoid unnecessary questions or leaks, I didn't mention to anyone that I had brought crews in from Los Angeles, including Rob.

Rob sensed I was hiding something from him and said, "If you ask my opinion, I suggest you bring a few of your…"

I stopped him.

"Rob, I know what I'm doing. Trust me and let me do things my way. To the best of my knowledge, I have yet to disappoint you."

"You're the boss," he answered without taking offense. "Valencia and I trust you to do the right thing. By the way, I talked with him about your fee and there's going to be a nice bonus if you bring the girl home unharmed. Now all you have to do is find her. Anything else I can do for you before I'm out of here?"

"Yes," I answered immediately. "It is very odd that I haven't met Mrs. Valencia yet. I assume there *is* such a person. What's her part in this *telenovela*?"

"Now you are really getting to the soap-opera part of the Valencia saga. Donna Maria, Valencia's wife, is what we call present-absent. She is mentally unstable and physically unhealthy. She goes in and out of hospitals, and I believe she has not been told of her daughter's kidnapping."

"How does her condition affect Valencia?"

"He takes care of her. Not personally, of course. She has a nurse, a maid and a psychiatrist. She is on all the drugs in the book. She gets everything she needs and more, but as you can imagine, he does not like to discuss her in public."

"Are there any other women in his life?"

Rob shrugged...

"We're not that intimate. I assume he has, but I don't know for sure. I definitely don't know who they are. All I know is that a few years ago, he had this big love story with a young dancer he met at a nightclub. It was in all the tabloids, but I don't know how it all ended. It happened before I started to represent him."

"What about Alfonso Ortega?"

Rob turned sharply toward me.

"Now I think you are going too far. Ortega is one of the richest people in Mexico. He is even richer than Valencia. He is well connected in upper levels of the government. His brother is the minister of commerce and industry. Even though there is a long rivalry, I want to believe that it's all part of the normal course of business. Also, if I am not mistaken, they are even distant relatives."

"I understand there was a big business issue that exploded lately?"

"Yeah, there was the "Panorama" thing. I heard about it even though I was not directly involved. I only represent his affairs outside of Mexico. To the best of my knowledge, Valencia bought a failing television channel, Panorama, for peanuts. Within a few months he paid a lot of money to buy all the talent from Metropolis, Mexico's most profitable network, which happens to be owned by Ortega. He took everybody, anchors, reporters, editors, as well as Ortega's personal secretary. However, I think it is now in the courts and the scandal part of this story is over."

He paused for a second.

"I don't know why you are asking about Ortega and Panorama. It is not likely that a man of Ortega's stature would stoop so low as to hurt a business rival in this manner, even in Mexico. If you ask me, the answers are much closer to home."

"What do you mean by that?" I asked. "Jorge Cortez? The man is repulsive. I agree that he is the classic immediate suspect, but he would have to be unbelievably stupid to get involved in this, and I don't think he is. It would be so obvious to suspect him that I think he would have to be crazy to do it."

"Look, it's just a gut feeling," said Rob, "but I'm not the only one who has it. I know that Valencia feels the same. You remember what we used to say? 'If it looks like a duck, walks like a duck and quacks like a duck, then it's probably a duck.' You have to seriously consider the possibility that he is behind it all."

"So how do you explain that Valencia has entrusted him with his own security, the security of his companies and even the investigation of the kidnapping?"

"I think he wants him close by so that he can keep an eye on his activities and make sure that he doesn't hook up with his business rivals to plot against him," Rob observed. "Don't forget that he is married to Mona, Valencia's oldest daughter. Whether he likes him or not, there is a very strong family commitment involved."

"Maybe the explanation is that Cortez holds his dear father-in-law by the short hairs with some vital information that could cause Valencia severe damage."

I turned to Rob to catch his reaction to my wild theory. To my surprise, he took it well.

"That may very well be the case. Even a strong man like Valencia has weaknesses, and maybe Cortez stumbled across one and is using it to his advantage in his relationship with the old man. As you have figured out, Cortez is a ruthless man, and this is *your* problem now. This is why you are getting the big bucks. By the way, Ethan, did you ever think you would be getting so much money for doing what you love?"

11.

As I learned to expect from her, Gila did not disappoint. By the time we met in the lobby of the Independencia Hotel where she was staying, she had already followed through with most of the instructions I had e-mailed her early that morning.

She took off her sunglasses and reported, "Ricardo went to pick up the van we reserved at Avis. I am waiting for his phone confirmation. I think we can get two or three hand guns very easily. I'm going to get them at a local gun shop. I went there earlier and introduced myself as a tourist wanting to hike the Sierra Madre Oriental, needing something to protect myself against bandits. He bragged that he could get me any kind of weapon I wanted. So tell me what you want and I'll get it there."

My appreciation for Gila had grown as I'd gotten to know her better. For seven or eight years, she was a detective with the Special Investigations Division of the Israeli Police Department. The training and the skills she was able to develop there turned her into a very experienced and analytic professional. Her most important assets were her methodological approach and her ability to perform under pressure and distress. There was even a time that I toyed with the idea of making her my business partner. However, as often is the case with good plans, I didn't follow through.

She was 28 years old when we first met at a Middle Eastern restaurant in Los Angeles over four years ago. Two friends of mine owned the restaurant. Whenever Rob or I would get homesick, we would go there for a traditional breakfast of hummus, a hard-boiled egg served with pita bread, olives, pickles and Egyptian-style beans.

The restaurant owner introduced Gila and I, as she was aware of my police background. She had recently arrived in Los Angeles to "check it out."

A few days later, I had an opportunity to use her expertise on a case I had in Florida. Although we were there on business, we enjoyed each other during those warm Florida nights as a break from the tedium of the case.

It was Rob's idea to offer her a partnership.

"If she is so good and you really trust her, you should ask her to be your partner. Otherwise, the day will come when she will have enough contacts and a reputation good enough to open her own agency. You really don't want that to happen, do you?" he'd asked me.

By the time I had made up my mind, she had to return to Israel for a personal matter. When she reappeared in Los Angeles a few years later, the partnership was off the table. I tried to use her in as many investigations as I could, especially those that required Spanish, her mother tongue.

I had last worked with her on a case in New Mexico about two and a half months ago. It was good to see her again. I was about to ask her what she had been up to, but then I saw Ricardo walking toward us.

Ricardo, a tall, thin man with hair past his shoulders,

smiled. "Hey, man."

He shook my hand.

"Jody told me you had a birthday yesterday. Congratulations!"

"Jody can't keep her mouth shut," I said, joking. "It's just another date on the calendar. What's up with you?"

Ricardo put his Nikon gently on the table and sat on the couch next to Gila, stretching his legs all the way forward.

He was the best photographer I had, punctual and accurate. And most important of all, he produced. You could count on him to get the shot you needed if it was at all possible and sometimes even when it was not. He worked with me as a freelancer, but he rarely worked with anyone else because I enjoyed having him around and thus kept him very busy. I loved his character—easygoing, laid back and modest. More than once Jody had to remind him to come and pick up the check that had been waiting for him for two weeks in the office.

Ricardo mumbled some answer to my question.

"I think it's time you told us why we are here having so much fun and what you want us to do. Judging from your e-mail, I understand that we have some major time issues," said the always-practical Gila.

I told them about the kidnapping, my meetings with Señor Valencia and Cortez. I explained Cortez's role in the case. I then outlined my strategy to buy time and my plan to expose the kidnappers by means of a forced meeting.

Gila looked puzzled.

"I think the chances of this working are somewhere between slim and none."

She was not a person who held back her opinions, and I liked that.

I nodded in agreement.

"I know, but we've got to try it. We have nothing to lose. I don't want to get to the stage of handing over the money and then realize that, once again, Valencia has paid for a corpse."

Gila looked at Ricardo who was not showing any emotion. He was playing with his hair, and both of us knew that this was as distressed as he gets about professional matters.

"Anyway, and this is where you people come in, I want to check if any of the Valencia mansion employees are involved. I tried to get one of you inside undercover, but it didn't work."

I turned to Gila.

"Ricardo and you will do the surveillance. Alejandro and Miguel will check those who you decide are suspects."

"Does that include the two you mentioned earlier, Valencia and Cortez?"

"I would love to get information on these two, but I think it would be wiser to focus on the smaller players where the chance of finding something is greater."

"Based on what you told us, this Cortez person sounds like the classic immediate suspect."

"Too classic," I said. "That's what's bothering me."

Ricardo picked up his camera.

"Based on what you've said, I think I will need a lot more film and developer. I need to do a little shopping."

"Where are Alejandro and Miguel?" I asked Gila as Ricardo was leaving. "I want them to start working right away. Oh, and another thing: Warn them not to do anything stupid. Tell them to report any problems they have to you immediately. If they get into any kind of trouble, tell them to break contact. I don't want any complications, especially not some of the unnecessary stunts these two have been known to pull. The police here are just waiting for an opportunity to get into this, and that will ruin all our chances of getting the job done."

It was six months ago that Alejandro, Miguel and I were involved in a situation that almost caused my career as a private investigator to end prematurely.

We were driving back to Los Angeles from a very successful assignment in Colorado. Able to locate a businessman who had pulled off a successful sting operation on four banks simultaneously, we were in high spirits. What excited us was not simply the successful completion of a mission, but also the prospect of getting a good night's sleep in a real bed after being awake for over 72 hours.

We were getting close to our destination when a truck cut us off sharply and almost forced us off the road. I lose my cool when stuff like that happens. I began to speed up until I caught up with the truck. Alejandro and Miguel, their upper bodies completely out of one window and the sunroof, started making obscene gestures at the driver, telling him about the occupation of his mother and other family members in fluent Spanish.

Unfortunately, 300 yards ahead were two highway patrol units, just waiting for something like this to happen. I had just enough time to tell Alejandro and Miguel that if the police asked, they were to say they didn't know me. They were just hitchhikers I picked up from Colorado on my way to L.A.

We went through the regular procedures: license, insurance, hometown, destination, etc. Then they asked me to open the trunk. I had no alternative. One peek inside the trunk made the acrobatics of Alejandro and Miguel no longer an issue.

All attention was drawn to the "treasures" in my trunk: sophisticated surveillance equipment, recorders, cameras, night vision and four guns, only two of which were licensed.

Alejandro and Miguel were able to convince the police that they were not connected, and they were released a few hours later. Rob got me released on bail a week later despite the objection of the prosecutor.

All the licenses and documentation I presented, including my membership card in the World Association of Professional Investigators (WAPI), my state of California investigator's license and some other professional affiliations had no effect. They were determined to view me as a terrorist, or alternatively as a *Mossad*, or Israeli intelligence, operative. Even though the only substantiated charge was illegal possession of firearms, they were adamant about prosecuting me on charges of plotting an assassination, as well as arms smuggling and trade.

The interrogation was intense. I was almost ready to accept the fact that I would spend the next two to three years in jail, and then have to find a new occupation when I got out. However, Rob, the magician, was somehow able to get me out of it with only a year suspended sentence and a $20,000 fine. To this day, I don't know the nature of the deal Rob struck with the federal prosecutor.

12.

Stevie caught me on the phone as I was getting into a cab back to the hotel. "Jody said I should call you on your mobile. I hope I'm not disturbing you. Am I?"

Stevie was a student, an acquaintance of Jody's. I'd hired him to help with the Hollywood producer's blackmail case. I had no doubt that the key figure in this case was Leo, the producer's young lover—a gay, handsome aspiring actor. It was hard to figure how, under the circumstances, an outsider could capture their intimate relationship on tape. It was much more likely that Leo had found a way to make his own home movies.

I wasn't mistaken. In a visit to his apartment (when he wasn't there), I found the tape. To my surprise, it was on a shelf in a conspicuous place among many others of the same nature. He did not attempt to hide the video documentation of his intimate encounters with various men. They were all labeled and dated. I also found the video-recording equipment, which Leo probably used to tape his performances.

These findings led me to the conclusion that it was indeed Leo who made the tape. However, someone else was doing the blackmailing, most likely without Leo's involvement.

After spying on Leo for a few days, Ricardo and I became familiar with his lifestyle. It was clear to us that if he had received the first $80,000 paid, it would have been reflected in his behavior. He probably would have moved out of his crummy apartment, bought a few new clothes and gone at least once to a decent restaurant. With great effort, I was able to gain access to his bank account. It revealed nothing that could be linked to the money paid by the producer.

Leo, living for the moment he would be discovered, spent most of his time auditioning. The rest of his daily routine included time at the gym where he obsessively worked on his physique and occasionally picked up a partner for casual and videotaped sex. In the evenings, he would occasionally visit a sleazy-looking gay bar called "The Pink Time" for drinks—a short walking distance from his apartment.

I decided to find someone who could get close to Leo. My theory was that someone he brought into his apartment saw the tape of him and the producer. He recognized the partner, figured that he could profit from it and was able to make a copy. It had to be someone who was close to him, not a one-night stand. Only someone with the same lifestyle as Leo had any chance of solving this case. That is where Stevie came in.

In the beginning, I was reluctant to give him this assignment. He was inexperienced and the case was very sensitive. I knew that failure could be very damaging to my reputation. That's Hollywood for you—one failure can erase a lifetime of success. Word of mouth is everything.

Otherwise, he was perfect for the role. He was a third-year art student, openly gay, a great body—tall, muscular and very manly. Jody said that when she and Stevie would hang out together, her women friends were devastated to learn of his sexual preference. The usual response was, "What a waste!"

Stevie practically begged for the job, and it was not just because of the money. When I showed him the pictures of the guys in Leo's life, the kind of men I wanted him to approach, his eyes almost popped out of his head. "I have never been paid for something I would love to do for free," he said, smiling like a teenager in love.

He proved himself valuable beyond all expectations. Without assuming a cover or changing his identity—an act that takes time and preparation—he was able to become a recognizable and favored character in "The Pink Time" crowd. It took only two days for him to get acquainted with Leo and visit his apartment. Two days later, he was already a member of Leo's gym.

He was in seventh heaven when he submitted his first report. It contained accurate information about many of the men currently in Leo's life. "It's my pleasure. Really, it is. Thank you very much for giving me this opportunity," he said with that smile of his.

The report had information about eight guys that Stevie nicknamed "Leo's Band of Merry Men."

"In your best judgment, who within this group would have a motive for blackmail?"

He paused for a minute.

"There are three maybe even four who would do anything for a quick buck if they found an opportunity. There's Rocky, an Italian male prostitute. This kind of money could change his world drastically. There is this guy that everyone calls 'The Piece'—he's named after his large genatalia. On a foggy day, you can't see its end. He got out of jail two years ago after serving four years. He had robbed a store and sent the owner to the hospital for 10 days in the process. Then there is also a guy named Eric.."

Stevie then pointed to a photograph of a skinny blond with the look of a martyr.

"This one is Leo's favorite. His name is Dan. They have a cat-and-mouse kind of relationship where Dan is playing Leo. I think he is a very dangerous, maybe even *sick* type."

I sent him back to work with the instructions to focus on the four main suspects, and an envelope with his pay: $600.

"So far you have acted like a real pro. My congratulations. Now it's time to really start working. I need to start providing my client with answers as soon as possible as to who is blackmailing him. More importantly, I need to make it stop."

"Anything else? I'm listening?"

"I need some advice, actually authorization," he said, embarrassed. I encouraged him to continue.

"I am really in a predicament here. I have developed a very good relationship with Eric, one of the four suspects. I have also made an effort to get close to Dan, the dude that will sell his mother for a few dollars, the guy Leo worships, remember? By the way, I heard he is in deep crap with debts and stuff."

"Stevie, please get to the point," I said impatiently.

"Anyway, Dan has the hots for me and has asked me to go spend the weekend with him in San Francisco. But, I have great chemistry with Eric and he says that if I go with Dan he will not speak to me ever again. By the way, if Eric weren't a suspect, I would be all over him by now."

I didn't know how to respond to this. Part of me wanted to burst out laughing. I was accustomed to my guys calling me for advice on personal matters, but this dilemma he was in was a first for me.

"Stevie, what do you want me to say?"
"What do you mean? Tell me what I should do." He was dead serious.

"I really don't know," he continued. "On one hand, I don't want to go with Dan because he's not my type. If I go with him then it's all the way, you know what I mean? Also, I lose Eric, and maybe even Leo if he finds out. On the other hand, I have a strong feeling that he is our guy. A weekend with him will allow me to find the proof that it's him."

I took a deep breath.

"How much is it going to cost me?" I asked, dreading his answer.

"Nothing, he's paying for everything. As you know, I'm just a poor art student. If he has the money for this, then it even increases the chances that he's the one. He is a slimy character, but he is so sexy and he takes advantage of his looks. He screws everything in sight. So, hey, why not have some fun?"

"Go, Stevie. Have a good time," I offered. "If you say that this is your gut feeling, then go with it. Go have fun. I mean…"

I felt uncomfortable and Stevie noticed it.

"OK, Ethan. I think it's the right thing to do. I will call you or come by the office when I return."

The second I finished this weird conversation with Stevie, the phone rang again.

"Hi. I'm leaving the library right now. When do you want to pick up all the information that I have so far? There are a lot of articles about these two lovely friends of yours."

"I would love to invite you to lunch. I haven't had anything to eat since…"

"Great, I'm starving. Where are you?"

"In a taxi, on the way to my hotel."

"Let me speak with the driver. I'll tell him where to take you. It's a small restaurant, very good food and not expensive, you will love their food."

13.

The small Mexican restaurant, Frijoles, was located not too far from the Museo Nacional de las Culturas on Moneda Street, and it lived up to Lisa's praises.

I can't remember myself ever enjoying such simple and basic food before. My favorite was *botanas*, a succulent mixture of red beans and chicken in a spicy sauce served with fresh tortillas. Tortillas reminded me a little of *laffa*, large sheets of pita bread served in the restaurants of Jaffa.

However, the most enjoyable part was reuniting with Lisa after almost 12 hours apart. For the first time since we met, I felt open and relaxed with her. Her warmth and affection made me less suspicious the more time I spent with her.

It is very hard for a man in my profession to ignore the saying that "if it appears too good to be true, then it probably is." The coincidental meeting in the library, her immediate willingness to help, the meeting in the restaurant and her acceptance of my offer to go out that same night were all very nice, but I could not get rid of the feeling that it was too well scripted, and perhaps, produced especially for me.

Being available and fond of pretty women made me very aware of the possibility of their being used against me. Many times I have stopped seeing women who made me suspicious, regardless of the pleasure I experienced in their beds. One time, I knew for sure that a date was thrown to my lap as part of a rival's plan. However, I stayed with her for two reasons. First, she was one of the sexiest women I had ever been with, and second, I used our relationship to provide her senders with disinformation to the benefit of my client. I do not like doing business that way even if it is effective.

In a financial investigation I conducted in Chicago, I used a French girl of Chinese descent, Lily, as bait to get inside information on my clients' rival company.

My clients, who had a major market share in the wholesale-meat industry, asked for extensive information on a new company that had begun to penetrate the market. The clients needed as much information as possible: profit-and-loss statements, client lists, financial resources, etc.

It took almost 10 weeks to gather what they asked for. They were pleased, but not satisfied. Their next assignment was for us to obtain ongoing updates on various activities.

My first inclination was to have one of my people hired to work with the rival company and provide the information. It was too lengthy a process, and we needed an inside person right away. Then I met Lily.

Like millions of others, she arrived to take Hollywood by storm. She found out the hard way that possessing a degree in psychology from a French university and a pretty face is not an automatic ticket to fame. When we met, she had been in Hollywood for over two years and had made no progress to write home about. She had a few jobs but always ended up working as a call girl. "It's the easiest money and the demand is always greater then the supply," she explained.

She came to mind as I was looking through the files of the four partners of the rival company. 'If I can attach Lily to one of them, it'll be great,' I thought to myself.

I called the clients to approve the additional costs involved and with no hesitation at all, they approved the operation.

"Go for it. Money is not a problem."

All Lily was interested in was how much she was going to get paid.

"You'll start at $1,000 per week. Once you are together, it will be $1,500 per week, plus $500 to $1,000 for any valuable information."

She accepted the offer.

"Who am I supposed to hook? I hope he's nice at least."

"I want us to decide this together," I told her. "Your psychology background can be very helpful."

Lily looked at the files and finally pointed to one of them.

"This is the one," she said with confidence.

She pointed to the file of the company's marketing manager, 48 years old, married and a father of three. He seemed to be a typical conservative workaholic, and whatever free time he had was dedicated to his family. He was the least impressive of the group, and my files had no interesting stories to tell about him.

I looked puzzled. She smiled.

"Trust me, I'm only 27 years old, but I know people and especially men. This guy will bring down the moon for a girl like me. I will need some time to find the right place and time to get him, but eventually he will be eating from the palm of my hand like a puppy."

Lily justified every cent she got paid. A little more than two weeks later, she reported that she had "closed on him," as she called it. A week after that, she already reported the company's development plan and the relationship between the partners. All her reports were professional and to the point.

This went on for six months. We met every two weeks for a morning cup of coffee or a late-night drink. In every meeting she presented very valuable information and an account of her relationship. The man had fallen head over heels for her and had bought her a car, rented her an apartment very close to the corporate headquarters and pampered her with expensive gifts every time they met. She enjoyed the arrangement.

Then the company that hired us wanted to hit their rivals directly. They had a plan. I needed to use the relationship with Lily to threaten the executive. He was to help bring down his own company, otherwise intimate photographs, which I was supposed to take, would be sent to his wife.

In my line of work strong morals and human compassion are not "necessary" virtues, however, professional ethics are a must. This demand was blackmail, and it crossed the line. My refusal to participate in their scheme led to an immediate end of our business arrangement.

"Thank you very much, Mr. Eshed. From this point, we will take care of things our way. It has been a pleasure knowing you."

What was going to happen next was clear. I have always felt a responsibility toward my employees and I had no intention of abandoning Lily. I called her, and 30 minutes after my being fired, we met in our regular coffee shop.

"The shit is going to hit the fan," I told her as I described the chain of events. "I would strongly urge you, as your friend and employer, to vanish. Not tomorrow, not in a while. Today, right now. These people are capable of anything. I think you have accumulated enough money to start fresh somewhere else."

Two months later, I got a call from her that she had moved to New York and was studying acting.

With this experience in mind, it was reasonable to suspect that Lisa was not a heaven-sent gift, but a ticking bomb that could explode in my hands any minute. However, the hours we spent together convinced me otherwise. It was too good to be false. It was too pretty to be a show.

I remembered what Dianne, my ex-wife, used to tell me: "You fuck, you don't make love." To be honest, at the time I had no clue what she was talking about. It took me a few years to grow up and feel that something was missing even when the sex was great. I started craving intimacy.

"You can't learn it. Either you've got it or you don't," Dianne said when I asked her to teach me how to make love. "It has to come from within, without planning. It just happens as a result of the way you feel."

That is how I felt with Lisa. Lisa showed me that even with Meeka I had just scratched the surface of the world of intimacy. If indeed Meeka and I shed some layers of superficiality, I now realized that it was almost always my doing. With Lisa, maybe for the first time in my life, I could love and be loved in return without boundaries.

"Since we said goodbye last night, I haven't been able to stop thinking about us," she whispered in my ear, kissing it gently. "I can hardly concentrate. I want you with every part of my body."

I hugged her.

"You can't imagine how much I want us to be together. I start to fantasize every time I think about it," I told her.

Her eyes sparkled as she whispered, "Wait for me in your hotel room. I will come to you after I finish my shift at the restaurant."

The waiter approached us with a fresh basket of warm tortillas and that stopped our whispering.

"Oh, I'm so stupid," said Lisa suddenly. "I almost forgot the most important thing."

She took a thick stack of papers clipped together out of her bag.

"This is what I had time for today," she said apologetically as she handed me the stack. "I hope it will be useful. There is a lot more where this came from. I didn't have enough time to translate everything word for word, so I summarized some of the less-interesting articles."

I pushed my plate aside. I looked briefly at the papers, and after only three pages, I knew I had made the right decision. The information, presented in delicate handwriting, was exactly what I needed.

"Excellent! This is great! Good job! If you can get me some more tomorrow and maybe the day after, it would be great."

"Tomorrow the library is closed because of the holiday, but the day after, I can do it."

"Should I pay you every day or when everything is done?" I asked.

"Don't be stupid. It is true that yesterday I was very happy to make some extra money, but now we are not in an employer/employee situation. Now I am helping you because you need help. What am *I* doing anyhow? Simply reading a few newspapers and translating articles. You want to pay me $100 a day for that? Forget it. I will not take one peso from you."

I leaned forward and kissed her forehead.

"What is happening between us has nothing to do with the great job you did. I really needed it done and if we hadn't met, I would have paid someone else to do it. I am very moved that you want to help me, but like I told you yesterday, I decide who I pay for what and how much."

"Let's drop it for now," she said in an appeasing tone. "I'm glad I can help you and I will continue to do so. It's a shame I can't be with you all the time while you are in Mexico. It's not just that I want to be with you 24 hours a day, but I could get to see a real-life investigation up close."

"I know it sounds interesting, but I am not sure that this job is suited for someone like you. There is a lot of dirt and danger. It could even kill you. It's not something to take lightly."

"There are many things that could kill you," said Lisa, "car accidents, earthquakes and even food poisoning in some of the restaurants in this country. When Jorge Cortez is around, you never know how it will end. Two separate articles regarding two different corruption stories in which he was involved reported that police investigators and officers mysteriously disappeared. Shocking and scary, isn't it? You need to be careful."

"I am always careful, and in this case, he is not the subject of my investigation. We are on the same side."

I started to feel uncomfortable with the direction the conversation was going.

"It's a very complex investigation and I am really not able to talk about it. Let's just enjoy the food."

"So it's probably about Valencia," Lisa continued anyway. "He's not a saint either. I found a story about an affair he had with a 21-year-old dancer who could have been his daughter. Instead, she made him a father."

I was tempted to dissect every page of the articles she had gathered for me right then and there. The information that Lisa casually dropped about the two new men in my life could be very significant investigation leads, and I needed to pursue them fast. I had to figure out what I had gotten myself into.

"You don't have to talk about it right now but can I be with you while you work?" Lisa asked insistently.

The alarm bells in my head started ringing again stronger then ever. Her explicit and persistent request to be involved in the investigation raised all the red flags and triggered all the defense systems. I didn't want this to be the case.

"Lisa, I'm sorry. It would be dangerous. The last thing I want is to put you in harm's way."

"Did you forget? I am not a coward and I like taking risks. Working with you could be the opportunity I am looking for to leave my father's house. Since I am not married, he will not allow me to get my own apartment in the city. Not *my* father. My sister ran away to America so she could live the way she wanted—free of him."

"Why don't you join her?" I asked.

"Someone has to stay with my mother," she said with obvious pain in her voice. "She is not well and I cannot leave her with him. He tried to hurt her. If it weren't for her, I would have been far away from here a long time ago."

14.

The phone rang at exactly 11:00 p.m. It echoed in the dead silence of Valencia's office. The show was about to begin.

I gave Cortez a sign to switch on the tape recorder as I picked up the special earpiece that we installed. Cortez, sucking on his cigarette, followed my every move. Valencia picked up the receiver.

"Speak normally," I had told him earlier. "Keep your cool, explain the situation and don't get angry. If you feel you cannot control yourself, take a deep breath. Her life depends on your response."

He did not answer. He seemed self-focused as he lowered his head. His anxiety was apparent and he was making every effort to shake it off.

"Explain that you want to pay, but due to the holiday, you need another two to three days to put the money together."

"*Hola.*"

"*¿Señor Valencia?*" I heard a man's voice ask.

"*Sí, habla el Señor Valencia.*"

Obviously, I understood very little of the conversation.

From Valencia's tone of voice and body language, I had a feeling that everything was going as planned. A sigh of relief from Valencia at the end of the phone conversation assured me that our goal had been accomplished quite easily.

"He is going to call back on Monday at the same time. I guess the holiday story made sense to him and he did not argue or threaten."

"It really was very quick," I said. "Did he try to suggest that you were stalling or anything like that?"

"No. It was as though he already knew what I was about to say. I think he already had his answers ready. I hope it's not a trick or a trap..."

Cortez interrupted him.

"I think there is no need for us to be surprised. These are professional criminals with experience in situations like this. They probably took into account a delay of a few days. I guess that happens for some reason or other in any kidnapping case where a large ransom is requested. You sounded very convincing and sincere, so it makes sense that they agreed to wait a few more days."

"Did you ask about Carmen?" I inquired.

"Of course," said Valencia as he took a long sip of water. "This was the first thing I needed to know. He said she is fine and being taken care of. He said that if I am true to my word, she would be home, healthy and safe, in no time."

"Was there anything else? Something that may help us identify the individuals involved? Something in the way they spoke, or the language they used, things like that?"

"No, there was nothing special. As you heard, it was a very short conversation. Like you said, I told him that we would not be able to get all the money because of the holiday, and that we would have to delay the whole thing for a few days. He didn't even try to argue."

"Was he the same man you talked to last time?"

"Yes, I believe so. I can't be sure, but I think he was. Oh, there was one thing. He said something I didn't like, but I was so focused on talking about the money and when it would be available, I guess I disregarded it at the time. He said that if I screwed him with the money, he would be on my tail for the rest of my life and that Carmen would be only the first chapter of what awaits me if he did not get his money."

The relief he expressed earlier disappeared in an instant. He looked as though he had aged 10 years in one minute. I had to encourage him and help him get a grip on himself.

I looked directly at him and said with confidence, "After we are done with these guys, they will not want to get near you. After we free Carmen, they will not be able to hurt anyone because we will have caught them."

He did not move. His posture gave away his desperation.

"It will not end with Carmen. It will not end with nine million dollars. They want to ruin me. Even if she comes back, they will continue to blackmail me. Life will become a constant hell."

Cortez came to life. He too realized that it was imperative to make the old man regain his self-confidence. His tone was sharp and clear. "He said that to scare you. They want you to be afraid so that you will do exactly what they ask you to do. It's the oldest psychological trick in the book, and they are playing it on you. I don't think you should take it so hard. There really is nothing to fear. He threatened—so what?"

Valencia looked at him. Cortez's words appeared to resonate well with him.

"Maybe you are right, now if you don't mind, I would like to be alone. Please excuse me."

15.

I arrived at my hotel room a little before midnight. Lisa was not there. She would have called if she were not coming. I tried to ease my anxiety, remembering she said that sometimes it took them over half an hour to clean up after the shift.

I decided to use the time to go over all the newspaper articles she had collected for me. I checked the room once again, using a sophisticated "Oscar" device to make sure no bugs were placed while I was away. Everything seemed in order.

I stretched out on the bed and read the articles one by one. Most of them were from the business and finance sections. There was also considerable interest in the gossip columns about the lives of Valencia and Cortez.

Generally, I never take newspaper articles too seriously. However, I realized that 'there is no smoke without fire.' In my current situation, every piece of information was valuable, even when the accuracy of the information was somewhat questionable. I made a mental note to ask Lisa to make sure all the articles were dated. This would allow me to put the information into perspective.

One of the more lengthy pieces dealt with the relations between Valencia and Amanda De la Vega, a very beautiful exotic dancer that held the stage name "Azúcar."

An article headlined, "Torn Between Two Lovers" told the readers that Valencia's decision to continue his relationship with Azúcar had to do with her being pregnant with his child.

"*The millionaire Diego Valencia bought a large house in Flamenco for his mistress, the exotic dancer Azúcar. Valencia is about to become the father of a son for the first time. The pressure from the Valencia family and the threats of his wife Maria, have had no effect on Valencia. He is not going to abandon the woman who is going to give him his first son after four daughters from a wife who he still refers to as the love of his life.*"

Another article dealt with the relationship between Señor Valencia and his wife.

"*It is not a secret that the impressive woman, who until recently was considered the number-one social hostess in Mexico City, has been suffering on and off for several years now from her medical condition. Her last two pregnancies were supposed to give her husband the male heir he so much desires. It is unfortunate for him that instead of the son he wanted, he now has two more daughters. At one time, the couple considered adopting a son, but that plan that was abandoned. The news of her husband's romantic relationship with Azúcar was delivered to Doña Maria in a mental clinic in the coastal town of Merida. Sources within her medical staff told our reporter that her situation has taken a turn for the worse and that currently she is in a deep depression and does not relate to her surroundings. To our question, 'Is her life in danger?' he responded, 'We are doing whatever we can and praying for the best.'*"

The next one was titled, "My Daughter is in the Hands

of a Great Man," and included an interview with Antonio (Tony) De la Vega, the father of the young dancer. The father did not seem to be bothered by the age difference between his daughter and her elder lover.

On the contrary, he was quoted saying, "*Señor Valencia is truly a great man and I am glad that my daughter has finally found a man who is most suitable for her. The fact that he is many years older than her and even a decade older than me, does not make a difference. Amanda is happy, and as a father, that is the only thing I care about. Amanda was always able to take care of herself and I am sure she will be as wonderful a mother as she is a dancer.*"

Another set of articles dealt with Jorge Cortez... 'El Halcón' or 'The Hawk' as the newspapers nicknamed him. One affair that had many references was labeled, "The American Sting." This amazing story seemed as though it came directly out of a Hollywood screenplay.

At the center of the story was Osvaldo, a Mexican arms dealer and partner of Cortez. Osvaldo was awarded a 57-million-dollar contract to supply arms to the Mexican military. It came as a surprise to everyone in the business that a relatively inexperienced company was awarded such large a contract. All the competitors questioned their ability to fulfill the contract at the prices quoted— over 25 percent lower than their closest rival. Cortez had left Valencia at the time and was trying to make it outside of his father-in-law's organization. He contacted an American company, Horizon. According to the article, they operated on the fringe of the law without official authorization from the government to trade in weapons and arms. Horizon promised to supply Osvaldo with merchandise at a very low price, and Osvaldo fell for it.

Horizon chartered a ship that carried the merchandise and unloaded the containers in a private harbor not too far from Mexico City. Osvaldo's executives signed for the shipment and authorized the transfer of funds, 32 million dollars in total, to Horizon. When the military came to pick up the containers, they found old, worthless equipment. The three signers on behalf of Osvaldo—all close allies of Cortez—disappeared, with the newly deposited millions in secret bank accounts they'd previously opened in Switzerland.

Osvaldo went bankrupt, and Cortez's legitimate partners who had lost fortunes in the deal ganged up on him and blamed him for orchestrating the scam. The courts did not find proof of Cortez's criminal involvement. However, the judge did reprimand him harshly for his behavior throughout the ordeal.

In an out-of-court compromise, Cortez agreed to pay a symbolic compensation of a few million dollars to his ex-partners. The money was paid by his father-in-law, and at his daughter Mona's request, Cortez was allowed to return to work at Bartelieu.

The story the newspapers called "The Clash of the Tycoons" was represented by eight lengthy pieces, which Lisa summarized for me. These articles dealt with the rivalry between Diego Valencia and Alfonso Ortega and the Panorama incident, which Cortez had already told me about.

The articles revealed a few interesting facts that Cortez did not mention, for instance, a past partnership that included the sports cable channel Noventa Minutos.

"*Señor Diego Valencia is no longer young, but his memory is still at its best, especially when remembering past insults from business rivals. It has been years since Alfonso Ortega was able, in what at the time was considered a brilliant business maneuver, to manipulate Valencia out of the extremely successful television network.*"

This is how the reporter described Valencia's cruel and elegant revenge:

"*The decision to get on the air with a channel broadcasting live soccer games was a public declaration of war. The planning was perfect and the execution was done in a military fashion. No one outside Valencia's organization knew what was about to happen. It was only when the first broadcast was already on the air that people in Mexico, including Ortega, realized that over 70 percent of the new channel's staff had worked the day before for Noventa Minutos, and that was just the first surprise. Discretely, without the media's attention, the Panorama people were able to close exclusive deals with major broadcasting networks in the U.S., South America and Europe. Furthermore, when representatives of Noventa Minutos wanted to extend existing contracts, they were told that someone had beat them to it.*"

"As of now," concluded the reporter, "*the Noventa Minutos channel is losing on all fronts. They have only two lucrative contracts remaining and when they are up for renewal in six months, they will probably go to Panorama, which has already released a statement offering almost double the price paid this year. So far, over 5.5 million viewers have switched to Panorama. It might very well be that Señor Ortega will pretty soon find himself with a network that has nothing to broadcast and nobody to broadcast it to.*"

"I Lost the Battle but Not the War" was the title of the editorial that analyzed Ortega's finances as a result of the Panorama situation.

"*It is still too early to write a eulogy for Señor Ortega's business career. His financial status continues to be sound in spite of the recent blow he received. All those acquainted with the tough businessman with ties to the highest levels of*

Mexican government know that he is not a quitter and that he is not a person to forgive and forget."

A source close to Ortega was quoted saying, *"Ortega vowed that he would take revenge tenfold regarding the 'sleazy and humiliating trick' that Valencia had played on him."*

Then there were a bunch of small items probably taken from society and gossip columns. I learned of Valencia's annual charity fundraiser ball to benefit Mayan heritage, held in the Tropicana Club, and of a donation of half a million dollars given to the preemie ward in a Mexico City hospital. There was an announcement telling the world about Doña Maria leaving the institute in Merida, and one about Señor Valencia hiring 35-year-old Nate Parker as his personal trainer. Next was an account of Mona and Jorge Cortez's lavish 20th anniversary party.

The phone rang.

"*¿Si?*" I answered in Spanish, hoping it was Lisa. But it wasn't; it was Gila.

"So, you've started speaking Spanish?"

"I'm practicing," I laughed. "*No hablo Español.* Yes, Gila, what's up?"

"I sent you an e-mail with a report on today's activities. Miguel and Alejandro are following two subjects: a woman named Nadia Morales and a man named Nate Parker. I don't know why I chose to start with them, maybe instinct. It's all in the report."

"Very good," I said. "I am going over some very interesting information. There are a few more people we need to check on, so we'll speak tomorrow morning and set up a meeting."

"I'm...I'm not really tired right now. I can come over, that is, if you want me to. Or you can come over here. You are more than welcome."

I was not expecting that at all. After the fondly remembered steamy nights in Florida, our relationship had been strictly professional. I believed it was destined to stay that way forever. "What's the matter?" I asked.

"Should something be the matter?" was her quick and impatient response. "You know, don't you? I'm in a good mood and I feel a little lonely, and I want some. So I thought that since we are here together, you know. It could be nice. What is it? I can't be open with you now? You always preach to us, 'truth and nothing but the truth.' It's good for everything and especially for sex, so…"

I was speechless and that does not happen often. My mind was racing trying to find the best way out of this awkward situation. I must say that the prospect of a night of wild and carefree sex with Gila was very appealing, but I was looking forward to a night with Lisa.

"Gila, Dear, I am really sorry, but I am so tired," I lied, slightly embarrassed. "I had a crazy day and I didn't get enough sleep last night. If I don't go to bed right now, tomorrow will be even worse."

"It's all right, Ethan. There's no need to apologize," she said. "I was just thinking, you know, for old time's sake. We don't have this opportunity every day, far from any commitment. You know, where we can exchange some sweat. You're the one who says that you only live twice."

I laughed. "I am really sorry. I know that the loss is all mine. Believe me, it is very hard for me to pass on that sweet sweat you are offering, but I am not even taking a shower. I'm going straight to bed. I'm exhausted."

"OK, I got it. You are not interested. It's fine with me. That means that I have to go down and find somebody else."

"You can do Ricardo."

She responded with a very relaxed and sensuous

laugh.

"Give me a break, Ethan. And I've also got Miguel and Alejandro. As you know, Dear, I like them fair-skinned and well developed, and none of these fellows matches the search criteria. But this is no longer your problem. You go to sleep and I will find myself an arrangement."

A few minutes later, there was a knock on my door.

"Who is it?" I asked trying to hide my anticipation. The voice on the other side was the one I was longing to hear.

"It's me. Lisa."

A second later, she was in my arms, my mouth passionately seeking hers and my hands caressing her body wildly.

"One second! Wait, wait!" She laughed, almost choking. She released herself, dropped her white handbag on the floor and just stood there smiling.

Her smile melted me entirely. Her green eyes gave me a teasing look.

"What's the rush?"

"I don't know. I've got to have you now," I said like an over-enthusiastic teenager doing it for the first time and not being able to hold back.

"I am not going anywhere, and believe it or not, we have the whole night to ourselves. Tomorrow is a holiday, and I told my father I am spending the night with a sick friend. I told my parents I will meet them tomorrow in the square."

I didn't really follow what she was saying. I stood there with my eyes wide open with admiration. She was stunning in a black mini dress that complimented her curves and looked like a marvelous extension of her shiny black hair. I followed the line from her graceful ankles to her sexy knees, and I had to stop myself from reaching for her again.

"I'm dying for a shower. I have been on my feet all

day. The restaurant was packed." She kicked off her high-heeled shoes. "Do you mind?"

"No, of course not. Do you want me to order something to eat? Or drink? Do you want some coffee?" I asked.

She did not answer. She unzipped her dress and it fell like a leaf in autumn and rested at her feet leaving her standing in the middle of the room in her blue G-string and matching bra.

She looked back at me as she walked toward the bathroom. "Would you mind washing my back?"

There wasn't anything to say. I followed her into the bathroom and stripped. I was excited and hard. She turned the water on in the shower and stepped in. Her soft skin smelled sweet as the hot water hit us. I kissed her mouth and neck as I held her breasts in my hands. Her nipples were hard, and she gasped when I put my mouth on them. Pulling my head back, she kissed me on the mouth passionately, and then, kissing me, she slowly moved her lips down my chest to my stomach. She put her hand around my erection, and then knelt down, grabbing my buttocks as she took all of me in her mouth. The combination of the hot water and her hot mouth on me was almost more than I could stand. She began taking me in and out of her mouth and licking the head with her warm, soft tongue. I moaned and grabbed her head as I came hard in her mouth. My knees buckled, and I almost collapsed on the shower floor. She held me tight, her head against my chest.

I picked her up and carried her out of the shower to the hot tub. As we sat entwined in the pulsing water, I became hard again. This time, it was all about her. I lifted her on top of me as I kissed her mouth deeply, and she moved until she collapsed against me. Then I turned and entered her from behind. We were soon spent, lying in the warm water, holding each other as if we would never let go.

16.

The sight was spectacular. Tens of thousands of people, from the very young to the very old, crowded the streets leading to La Villa de Guadalupe.

Some made their way somberly toward the two basilicas—the old one and the newer one built in 1976. Others just stood there in groups singing to the music of different bands at the corners of the wide-open plaza.

The old basilica was very impressive, designed in the style of the Italian Renaissance, and featuring a huge dome flanked by two towers. Lisa said it was built in the 17th century and for many years was a place of pilgrimage for hundreds of thousands of Mexicans from all around the country. Mexicans boast that it is one of the largest cathedrals in the world.

Following Lisa's advice, we decided to walk toward the new basilica—an enormous round structure designed in a modern style.

"It was built in 1976," she explained, "to accommodate the growing number of visitors and pilgrims. The new building can accommodate 40,000 people or more."

"Come," she commanded suddenly and grabbed my hand. "My aunt has a small restaurant nearby, overlooking the area. We can sit there and watch everything without being in the crowd."

A few minutes later, we were standing in the middle of a small restaurant called 'Pare Allí.' A heavyset woman wearing a white poncho smiled warmly as she saw Lisa enter. The two women, who were so different from each other, embraced warmly.

"Ethan, I want you to meet my aunt Babette, the person I love most in the entire world. She knows me better than anyone, even better than I do."

I shook her hand. She had a friendly, welcoming smile.

"*Hola, Señor.* I welcome you to this small place of ours. Every friend of Lisa is a welcomed guest here. Now, hurry and take a seat near that window. It is the best place if you want to see what is happening outside."

We sat on a wooden bench by a small table, and indeed, as Babette said, we could clearly see the waves of people below us. Men, women and children, most of them dressed in white, poured from the streets in what seemed like an endless stream.

To my surprise, despite the enormous number of people, everything was orderly and with no visible problems. Maybe the cooler-than-usual temperature had chilled the emotions and religious fervor and helped maintain civic order.

The most moving part of the whole scene was watching men and women crawling on their knees as they approached the church. Lisa said that they sometimes crawl for a mile to the church before entering.

"That is the tradition of our people. They are the penitientes," people who have asked the Virgin for a blessing or healing and come in prayer to the church on their knees to prove their gratitude and devotion," Lisa said, answering my puzzled look.

I looked at her as she sat on the bench a little closer to the window than I. She was completely taken with the whole scene below. Every so often she turned to me to explain things she thought might look odd to a foreigner like me. For a moment, I turned from a professional hired for a dangerous job into simply an incredibly happy man sitting next to an amazing woman, marveling at the sights and traditions of a strange and fascinating culture.

I hugged her, and she relaxed against me, her silky hair caressing my cheek. I don't ever remember feeling as relaxed as I felt with her.

"You do not know how happy I am that I'm here with you today," I whispered in her ear.

She turned her face to me. Her eyes sparkled.

"Oh, Ethan. I will tell you something that you might not believe. You might even think it's just a superstition. Promise you won't make fun of me."

I nodded and smiled. "I swear by the Virgin of Guadalupe."

Lisa was dead serious. "I swear by *la Virgen de Guadalupe* that last year I prayed to her asking her to send me a man who would make me feel like I feel with you. I know that it might sound stupid and primitive to you, but it has happened. She sent you."

I kissed her lips. The Virgin sent me here to meet Lisa.

Sometime in the middle of our incredible night in my hotel room, I made a decision to let Lisa know the truth about why I was in Mexico City. I decided to put my faith in the love of this woman. I trusted her. It wouldn't be possible for someone to fake the emotions she showed.

"I want to be with you all the time," she said, lying beside me while her hand gently stroked my chest. "I want to be part of the things you are doing here. Why can't you make me a part of your work here?"

"I *am* making you a part of it," I said. "You are helping me, more than you can imagine. I hope that the information you bring after the holiday will be…"

"That's something anyone can do, even a 13-year-old who knows a little English. That is not what I mean when I ask you to let me get involved. I want to know what's really worrying you and what you think about all the time. I want to know what it is and help you find a solution. That's what I mean when I ask to be part of you, part of your work."

"When I'm with you," I said softly, "nothing worries me, but I can't think of how you can help me."

She separated herself from me and, leaning her head on her hand, she grinned.

"Don't lie to me. I know you well enough to know that you are trying to be relaxed but you are really tense. You are warm and loving with me; attentive to everything I say and do. That gives me a great feeling, but at the same time, you are always watching, as if you are afraid something will creep up from somewhere. When we sat in the coffee shop, you sat with your back to the wall, facing the entrance. You eyed every person who entered, just like in the manual."

I was surprised that she had noticed my behavior. I do it without thinking anymore. I tried to be casual, telling her that she was exaggerating and had seen one spy movie too many.

"And, that big black bag you are hiding under the bed! I saw it last night when I picked up a hairpin that had fallen. Every time you open the door for me or for room service, you keep your body away from the door."

"You really do watch too much television. Only on TV is everyone a suspect. And if I intended to hide that big black bag, you wouldn't have been able to find it."

She laid her head on my chest and softly kissed my arm. "Maybe I went a little overboard, but I notice things that others don't pay attention to—things that make me wonder. I was told that I could be a very good investigative reporter, or detective, or something like that. Now tell me seriously, Ethan," she said, looking directly at me, "why don't you want to let me in on what you are doing?"

I stood firm.

"Because right now nothing is happening, and when something happens, it could become very dangerous. The more I know you, the less I want to put you in any kind of trouble. In a week or two, or maybe in a month, I will have finished my job here and will leave. You have to stay here and live among people who might not like what I have done to them. They may very easily hurt you if you become part of the situation. This is one responsibility I don't want."

She stood quickly. Bending down, she put her face near mine.

"I think you don't trust me," she said sadly. I see it. I feel it. You don't trust me, not really. You feel good with me, and it is obvious you want me, but then you think, 'Who is this girl? Where did she come from? What is she doing here with me?' You do not trust me, and you cannot comprehend that I am just Lisa and nothing else. You can't accept that I am here because yesterday, I liked you and today, I love you, and that's it. I guess you have been in this line of work for too long and you no longer have faith in people."

I smiled at her because that was all I could come up with. There was nothing I could hide. She could see everything.

"It is so strange that you don't trust me," she continued, "because you can't imagine how much I trust you. Just being here with you is an act of trust. Do you know what my father would do to me if he found out that his little daughter was having sex with a stranger, an *American*, a *Jewish* American, in a luxurious hotel suite? If you want to get rid of me, all you need to do is let my father know about tonight or send him a picture of me."

I was still smiling, feeling somewhat paralyzed by her total honesty.

"Let's make a deal," she said as she sat down suddenly. "I have a proposition that should make any doubt you have about me vanish. Take nude pictures of me with you, in any pose you desire, and keep it in case you need to get rid of me quickly. Just send it to my father and I'm history. Let's do it now! How about it? You see how much I trust you? Do you get it now?"

Instead of answering, I stretched my arms and put them around her waist.

"Come to me," I whispered.

I pulled her to me, and our lips met. The kiss was tender and the disappointment from a few minutes ago was gone. She closed her eyes and sighed, "*¡Ay, dios mío!* You drive me crazy! I can't even talk to you!"

There we were, sitting side by side in Aunt Babette's restaurant, looking at the commotion down in the street and enjoying ourselves like children.

Truthfully, although Lisa described the pageant as an "incredible cultural experience, not to be missed," I was more interested in watching this beautiful woman and thinking about our night together.

I learned from Lisa that in 1531, according to tradition, the Virgin of Guadalupe appeared four times at this exact place in front of Juan Diego who was a native Mexican. He had converted to Christianity just six years earlier. Legend had it that the Virgin commanded him to cover a robe with petals of *las rosas de Castillo*, and there her image would be revealed as proof of Juan Diego's vision.

Lisa continued, "Anyway, that was how Juan Diego was able to prove to the bishop, Juan de Zumarraga that he indeed spoke on behalf of the Virgin. She commanded him to welcome the natives warmly to Christianity. That led to the erecting of the basilica and the beginning of the pilgrimage to this place where people still come to ask the Virgin to fulfill their wishes."

My phone interrupted Lisa's story.

"Yes?" I barked into it, trying to ignore all the surrounding noise. I could read from Lisa's facial expression that she sensed that our time together there had ended.

"Ethan?"

"Yes, who is it?"

"Ricardo."

According to procedure, only Gila was supposed to communicate directly with me.

"Tell me, Ricardo," I tried to keep a calm tone. Lisa moved herself closer and hugged me as if trying to protect me with her body.

"They arrested Gila. I think it was the Mexican police. They took the van too."

"They arrested Gila?" I clenched my teeth and swore silently. That was not part of the plan.

"Where are you now?" I asked.

There was no answer. I quickly disconnected, praying that nothing had happened to Ricardo and hoping he would have the sense to call me back as soon as possible.

Lisa's worried voice interrupted my thoughts.

"Ethan, what happened?"

I looked directly at her, wondering what I should do

now.

"I need to go now. Something has come up. I have to take care of things. Now. Immediately."

She put her finger against my lips. "You don't have to justify your actions. It's all right. I'll come with you. I'll just ask Aunt Babette to tell my parents that I can't meet them. She will know how to explain it to them."

Holding her face in my hands, I said, "I'd rather you stayed here. Don't change your plans because of me. I'm sorry this is happening, but you do understand this is something I have no control over. Please call me after you finish here."

"You really don't want me to come with you?"

"No. I would prefer it if you stayed here. I know you understand," I said as she shut her eyes and lowered her head. I kissed her and looked into her eyes.

"Do you know how happy I am that I met you?"

She pushed me away.

"Go now. Be careful. I will call you later. Say goodbye to Babette on your way out. She is probably making us something to eat."

17.

The fear in Ricardo's voice was evident when he called back a few minutes after I left the restaurant.

"It was like in the movies. I got out of the van and walked away to get a better angle when suddenly I heard sirens. Four patrol cars surrounded the van and at least 20 police officers with submachine guns and pistols came out. Man, it was like Chicago in the good old days, but it was Mexico City of today."

"Spare me the drama. Someone might be listening. Are you sure none of the policemen caught sight of you?" I asked as I climbed the stairs to the street above the station.

"Yes, I'm sure. I took cover behind a garbage pile, and they didn't even think of searching there. I decided not to go back to the hotel, you know, in case they were waiting for me."

"Good. Have you heard anything from Alejandro and Miguel?"

"Gila told me she gave them the photos I shot yesterday. Do you want me to check on them?"

"No, I will do it myself," I said, waiving to a green taxi which stopped immediately.

"I need you to quickly develop everything you have and call me when you're done. Check into another hotel and stay there. I will call you; don't move till I do."

I asked the cab driver, a skinny guy in dark sunglasses to take me to El Presidente. As I was looking for Miguel's number, my phone rang again.

"Señor Eshed?" I immediately recognized the voice of Jorge Cortez. "I am very sorry to be disturbing you. It is a holiday, I know. I tried the hotel and there was no answer, and since you gave me your cellular number, I allowed myself…"

I knew exactly why he called me, but still, I tried to seem amused by his wit and provide some of my own.

"To what do I owe the honor of this phone call on your holiday?"

"We might have a slight problem," he said trying unsuccessfully to fake embarrassment. "I thought this might interest you. A few minutes ago, I got a call from the police. They said that they confiscated a van loaded with surveillance equipment just outside the mansion. Can you still hear me?"

"Yes, I hear you loud and clear," I said with an effort to show lack of interest, "and did they arrest anyone?"

"Yes, they did. My sources at the Mexico City P.D. told me that a woman was arrested. She claims she's just a tourist and that she doesn't have a clue what they want from her, but she was not able to explain the maps, binoculars, sophisticated photography equipment, surveillance microphones and other items not so typical for an innocent tourist."

"That sounds very interesting," I said indifferently, visualizing Cortez with his legs up on the table, a cigarette stuck in his mouth, and a huge smirk on his face. As hard as it was to admit, he had a very good reason to be satisfied. He had some major winning cards up his sleeve.

He continued, "The police assumption is that she was not working alone. They suspect she had at least one partner if not more, and they are now trying to locate them."

"Do they know who this woman is?" I asked.

He was waiting for this question.

"Oh! This is exactly the reason I had to call you so urgently. You would never believe the passport they found on her. Do you want to guess or should I tell you?"

I had to stop myself from not telling him exactly how I felt about his mother and his sadistic pleasures. He really enjoyed toying with me, and I had no other alternative but to play along.

"I am not in the mood to play 'Wheel of Fortune' with you, so please save me the trouble of guessing, and tell me."

I could hear him take a deep breath like a matador going for the kill.

"You won't believe this, or actually, maybe you will. The girl they arrested is named Gila. I hope I am pronouncing it correctly."

He was waiting for a response. I didn't give him the pleasure.

"Mr. Eshed, are you still with me?"

"Yes, I am."

"Excuse me. I thought we were cut off. To make a long story short, they started questioning her and she was saying all kinds of things—that she is researching Mayan heritage, and so on. When they asked her to identify herself, she pulled out an Israeli passport. Interesting, isn't it?"

"That is very interesting, and strange, very strange. We need to find out what she is doing there. Where did you say they picked her up?"

Jorge Cortez answered quickly, "Just outside the mansion. Only a few hundred yards from the gate, but let me run this wild idea I have by you. Can it be that the Israeli *Mossad* has any interest in Señor Valencia?"

I fired back quickly, "Señor Valencia probably knows more about that than I do. If I am not mistaken, you have even more information than he does."

There was silence on the other end of the line.

"Señor Cortez? Are you still there?"

Now it was my turn to have some fun.

"Yes, yes."

He regained his composure.

"I'm trying to think. I want to be frank with you, totally frank, Mr. Eshed, and you don't have to answer this, but I am really trying to be fair…you know…if these are by any chance, your people…"

I didn't answer, letting him play his game.

"Are you listening? I said, in case these are your people, I mean, people you called in to help with our case…you know…I have good contacts with the police and it isn't a problem to expedite their release."

At this point I had to take a risk.

"Señor Cortez, I really appreciate your concern, I really do, but I do have to disappoint you. I have nothing to do with this story. I don't have a clue about who she is. Believe it or not, there are millions of Israelis I do not know personally. However, as an Israeli, if this girl is not into drugs and did not do anything criminal, I think it would be very good for you to release her."

Apparently, this was not the answer he was expecting.

After a long hesitation he said, "Yes. I thought so."

At that point, I started getting tired of the game. I had better things to do than to play cat and mouse with Jorge Cortez.

"Mr. Cortez, I really appreciate your offer to help. It is very noble, and I am truly grateful even if it is for nothing. Hello? Hello? Are you still there?" And I hung up on him.

I hoped that he would think we had been disconnected. Even if he realized I had hung up on him, I didn't much care. Let him think whatever he wanted.

18.

I took a long sip from the bitter Mexican beer I was holding and looked around. I had a full view of the coffee shop through a huge mirror on its east wall. At this hour of the afternoon, it was full of young tourists and locals.

Lisa chose Café Ecstasy, insisting we meet before she had to start her shift at the nearby Barbarosa.

"It's a very popular place," she explained over the phone. "You can't miss it. It's a place for anyone looking for action."

It looked like a meat market—crowded, noisy and sweaty. I did not envy those youngsters, as they had to put a lot of energy into trying to sell themselves there. I tried to ignore the hubbub surrounding me and thought back to my meeting with Miguel and Alejandro that took place an hour earlier in the lobby of the Imperial Hotel.

I opted for a face-to-face meeting as opposed to a phone call mainly because I wanted to update them on Gila's arrest. My earlier phone conversation with Miguel revealed the anxiety and desperation they felt, and I knew it was as much my obligation to them as an operational need for the mission ahead to reevaluate and adjust to the changing circumstances.

"We are taking care of Gila, and I believe that within 24 hours she will be released," I announced with confidence as we sat at a corner table in the shabby hotel lobby.

They did not ask how things were being taken care of, as I didn't ask Rob when he assured me he was taking care of everything.

I did not tell them that I had promised Rob to send home everyone whom I'd brought in.

In a tone reserved only for the most dramatic of moments, he told me, "Take everybody out. Now! I don't know how you plan to continue, but if you don't want this incident to repeat itself, then you must tell everyone you have here to pack their belongings and take the first plane out of the country."

I was not willing to accept this demand. I felt the blood rushing to my head.

"So how the hell do you want me to work? The only reason I stalled everything was so that my people could do their work."

Rob was not impressed with my outburst.

"It was hinted that it was not a coincidence that Gila was arrested. Someone informed the police about the activities of the surveillance team. I don't think we should continue this conversation. I believe you know what I mean and understand how things came down."

I didn't want to push him. It was enough for me to know that Gila was being taken care of. I figured that Valencia had something to do with this. Who else could get the high levels of the police to react so fast?

"Good. Now what do you have for me?" I asked Miguel and Alejandro.

"Based on Gila's instructions, we focused on three individuals," said Miguel. "The first one is the old man's driver, Antonio Mendoza. The second one is Nate Parker, Valencia's personal trainer. The third one's name is Sonia Durazo, who, as far as we know, is the wife's private nurse."

"Skip the introductions," I said impatiently. "What did you find out?"

Miguel was not happy that I'd cut his prepared presentation, but he did not argue. "On the last one, that Sonia woman, we don't have anything yet. We need a few more days. About the driver, according to a conversation Alejandro had with a friend of Mendoza, who also used to be the old man's driver, this Antonio is loyal to the man like a dog. He would die for him. He feels he owes him his life. This Antonio used to be a very famous soccer player who got involved with drugs and Valencia saved him, or something like that."

"Got it," I said. "What about the third one?"

Miguel looked at Alejandro and then back at me.

"We found something that we think is interesting. When Gila and Ricardo told us he was leaving the mansion in his brand new silver four-by-four Jeep, we tailed him. He drove to his house. He's a good-looking man—long blond hair, muscles, tan, the works—you know the type. Anyway, about two hours later, three girls went into the house which is not something unusual with him looking the way he does, and..."

Alejandro interrupted him.

"Miguel, excuse me, but I think it is important to note that the girls...I mean, I know that sometimes Mexican women look young for their age, but these were really young, I think under 16."

"As always, you are exaggerating," said Miguel

annoyed.

I hushed them both.

"16, 17, 18...OK, so this guy is a maniac and is into young girls."

Alejandro nodded, "To be honest, he does look like a maniac. And how can a trainer afford a house like that, and the Jeep and the whole life style he has going? If you ask me, with all the macho performance the dude is a *maricón*, a queer. I smell these types from a mile away."

"You drive me *crazy*, where do you get that from? Or maybe you have the hots for him or something like that," quipped Miguel sarcastically.

Alejandro, filled with anger, replied, "If you really want to know, it's your little sister whom I have the hots for. I would love to screw her. And if you really want, I will do you for dessert!"

"Enough! Stop it!" I yelled, tired of their nonsense. "You two are acting like babies!"

They always did that. After every assignment, I would promise myself not to rehire them, but I always ended up calling them eventually. These two bachelors in their mid-30s were a great team. They could handle almost any curveball thrown at them. Their love of life and its pleasures, coupled with their hot tempers, did not make them less professional—just a little bit more annoying at times.

Their unit in the New York Police Department begged them to stay on the force regardless of the countless complaints against them for misconduct.

Both of them left the N.Y.P.D. at the same time and have stayed together ever since. They decided to take a long vacation in Los Angeles and that is when they thought to call me.

We met a year earlier in New York. I was conducting

an insurance investigation, and our paths crossed. I came to like them and was impressed with their skills. "If you ever get to L.A.," I had said, "I would love to buy you dinner and show you around." We had exchanged numbers and they promised to call.

As promised, we went out for dinner. Los Angeles—the sun, the beaches, the babes and the luxurious cars—drove them crazy. "We've decided to stay," they told me. "We rented a small apartment in Malibu, on the beach, and we're kicking ass. We deserve to live it up after eating shit for 10 years on the streets of the Bronx and Harlem, don't you agree?"

I used to visit their 'house of sin,' as they referred to their apartment. I loved their ocean view, but I didn't really get excited about the girls who hung around there all the time. Eventually, they spent all the savings they had accumulated and were forced to get back to work. I was more than happy to use them whenever I could.

Their childish behavior and their professional expertise came as a package deal—take it or leave it. I took it and had to endure their being impossible and irritating just as they were at this exact moment. Their natural warmth and easygoing demeanors allowed them to forge personal contacts in no time, and use them to gather information. They could blend in with any crowd in seconds.

Probably the best demonstration of their talent was in an investigation we did together in Florida. We had arrived there to find a married, 50-year-old businessman who had fraudulently obtained loans from several banks and left town before repaying them. The only lead I had when I got the case was the name of his lover, a 20-year-old Swedish student, who attended a Florida college.

I sent Miguel and Alejandro after the Swedish boy. We found out that his favorite pastime was hanging out at one of the nearby beaches. It took them fewer than three hours to become friendly with him. Their cover was of a madly-in-love couple.

The same night the three of them went out to one of the gay clubs in town. Miguel was shocked to find the Swedish guy flirting with him. He played along, pretending to make Alejandro extremely jealous. The next morning, we knew the whereabouts of the runaway businessman.

"But that is not what we wanted to tell you," said Miguel, his voice bringing me back to the present. "The interesting part happened yesterday around noon. At approximately 12:05 p.m., a black Land Rover stopped by the house, and who slipped in quickly not wanting to be seen?"

I looked at him with curiosity. Miguel smiled.

"I knew you couldn't guess. Believe it or not, it was our patron, Señor Valencia!"

That really was a surprise.

"Was he alone? Were you able to find out what went on inside?"

"No, sorry. We weren't set up yet to see what was happening inside. He stayed there for an hour, not more. Antonio, the driver, stayed in the car. After about an hour, the old man came out, got into the car and they drove away.

19.

It is sometimes the naïve bystander, the one not personally attached to a version of the past and how things should work, who can see things in a second that a whole panel of experts could never see. That is exactly what happened when I revealed the whole kidnapping story to Lisa that afternoon at Café Ecstasy.

"If you do not make direct contact with the kidnappers, you will not be able to track them down. Why don't you push them to show you Carmen, physically, that she is really alive and in good health?" she asked.

I voiced my usual concerns, even though I knew she was right.

"They agreed to extend the deadline because they understood that it takes time to put together such a large sum. But that does not mean they will risk exposing themselves face to face. There are more ways than one to prove that she is alive. They can send a picture or a video with her holding a dated newspaper or something like that."

Lisa insisted.

"You should make it an imperative condition. If there is

not a visual confirmation, then no ransom will be paid. You can say that after the experience with Mariana, Valencia is afraid that the minute they take the picture, they will kill her. You need to be tough and go with it all the way. If they think that they might lose the money, they will take the risk of a meeting. Do you know what nine million dollars means to these people?"

I continued to play devil's advocate even though I agreed with every word she said.

"They would be stupid to agree. If I were them, I would immediately assume it's a trap."

"You don't know who they are. Maybe they are stupid. Maybe they are not as professional as you believe they are. What have you got to lose? This is the only way to get to them. Based on his past experiences, it makes sense that Señor Valencia would not be willing to take any chances. He could also tell them that he has already accepted the worst-case scenario that Carmen will not be coming back, so as far as he is concerned, the pressure is on them. No meeting—no payment."

I smiled, not revealing that this was exactly what I had planned to do in Monday night's phone call.

"OK, you convinced me," I said. "All we need to do now is convince Señor Valencia. I don't really know if he is going to like the idea. As you probably understand by now, he is not a very easy client. I am going to throw him a little bait."

Lisa looked at me intrigued. I smiled a mysterious smile.

"Don't ask me now what it is. It's just a simple trick, and if it works, more than half of the job will be finished. It will be one giant step for the investigation. I promise to tell you everything later."

Lisa accepted that.

"I'm not going to pressure you now and I don't intend to do so in the future. Tell me when you want to. The most important thing is that I am with you. That is all I want."

I gazed at the beautiful young woman sitting in front of me, resting her chin in her hands. I couldn't be sure that what I was feeling was love, but I really enjoyed every second I spent with her. She took in every word I used to describe my adventures of the last few days. Her eyes were fixed on mine and she gasped in astonishment as she listened.

I couldn't help comparing Lisa's total interest in everything I told her to Meeka's courteous attentiveness. It was the genuine care that made the difference. Meeka listened to everything I said because she felt it was part of her role as a companion. Lisa made me feel that everything I said was important to her. It was important to her because it was important to *me*.

Her input helped me reevaluate the contents, and the way I might approach Valencia on this issue.

Lisa peeked at her watch and placed her hand on mine.

"I'm sorry Ethan. It's late and I want to be on time for work. Please ask for the bill."

We walked down the wide pavement toward Barbarosa. The warm wind contrasted remarkably with the dark clouds above. One by one, the neon signs flickered on. The street was grooming itself for another busy night. The coffee shops were already filling with men and women, some very young, and others trying to *look* very young, wearing the latest styles and fashions.

I noticed a young man, tall and skinny, walking parallel to us on the other side of the street. I had seen him earlier, standing at the bar counter at the 'Ecstasy.' I was sure it was the same person. His white T-shirt had attracted my attention for some reason.

I continued to walk, considering whether to try to lose him or lure him into an alley and take care of him there. I didn't know if he was alone, but I knew what to do.

"Wait a second," I told Lisa. I bent down and started fidgeting with my shoelaces. Lisa did not suspect anything. I envied her, living in a world in which you are not constantly looking over your shoulder. The young man stopped on the other side, confused. I looked down, and when I lifted my head, he was gone. I took Lisa's hand and pulled her.

"I really hope that I am not getting you into trouble. I think that someone was following me, and if this is the case, now they also know about you."

She pushed her body against mine, her breasts pressed against my chest.

"Now they know that we're together. As far as I am concerned, they can explode. I really hope that whoever is following us reports to Cortez, and that he is jealous of you."

I took her head in my hands and kissed her gently.

"I don't want anything to happen to you."

She pulled away with a smile. "You worry too much. Nothing is going to happen to me. You cannot imagine how happy I am that you finally let me into your world. I don't know if I have been of any help to you, but I already feel a part of you. I really do. Mr. Eshed, you make me happy."

I hugged her. And right behind her, I saw the man in the white shirt.

20.

I considered my next step for a while and eventually, I had my game plan in place. With the help of the hotel's desk clerk, I called Barbarosa and asked to speak with Lisa.

It took a while, but then I heard her voice, "*Hola. Habla Lisa.*"

I purposely spoke in a distant tone.

"Hi, this is Ethan. Don't respond immediately. Hear me out, and then decide. If you think you don't want to do it, it's all right. But I would be very happy if you could help me."

"No question about it, Ethan, what do you need?"

I heard her enthusiastic voice and I raised my voice slightly.

"Lisa! Please listen first before you give your answer. I can't go into details over the phone, but I need you to come to my hotel as soon as possible. Can you do that?"

There were a few seconds of silence.

"The truth is, I will try. Do you need me for the entire evening? I mean, do you think I will be able to return? I need to tell them here."

"Lisa, you really don't have to do this. If you say you can't, I'll understand. However if you can come, even for an hour, it would be good. There's been a little problem, and I need some help."

"I'm coming. It will only take me a few minutes." She hung up the phone.

Finally, I had time to take care of myself. I looked at myself in the bathroom mirror. My nose was still bleeding and a bluish-purple bruise had started to form on my cheek just under my eye. My jeans and my favorite T-shirt were bloodstained.

"Shit," I mumbled. "I hate when these things happen."

I gently washed my aching face and took off my clothes. Wearing only my boxer shorts, I exited the bathroom and walked toward the closet, ignoring the pleading look of the curly-haired man tied up to the armchair by the bed. I took out a clean pair of jeans and a brand-new black T-shirt. I sat on the bed in front of my laptop as the cuffed man followed my every move.

Two hours earlier I had said goodbye to Lisa in front of Barbarosa and decided to walk back to the hotel. I had hoped that the young man was still following me but he was nowhere to be found. I really wanted to know who had sent him.

I walked the main street observing the variety of characters parading in the streets. At some point, I entered El Niño Café. It had a view of the row of hotels that included El Presidente.

I was sipping some coffee slowly trying to see if anyone was following me when the phone rang. It was Gila.

"Hi. They released me a minute ago," she said. If she was excited or nervous, you could not tell it from her voice.

"Hey, Gila! Are you OK?" I on the other hand, did not try to hide my happiness at hearing her voice.

"How did they treat you? How are you feeling?"

"I am OK, thanks," she said in the same tone. That was as far as she spoke about her condition.

"I understand that I should take a plane to Los Angeles as soon as possible. Correct?"

"Yes, I think it is the best thing to do. Take a few days of paid vacation. We will take care of the money issues when I get back. I'm sorry it ended this way…"

She interrupted me.

"No. I wasn't as alert as I should have been. I guess my age is starting to show. Truth be told, the police were courteous and gentle. They didn't push too hard. I think it was more important for them to get me off Valencia than to know exactly what I was doing and for whom. They, of course, know what they need to know. You understand?"

Of course I understood. Gila gave them the story we agreed upon before we began the surveillance.

"I am very sorry it ended this way."

"Forget it. The most important thing is that you're out. Don't worry. I will be OK and we will get the job done."

"I do have something for you. It sounded like gossip, but I think it is worthwhile to check it out. The police didn't remember I spoke Spanish, or didn't care, but I overheard the two officers speaking about Valencia and a Tony De la Vega. Does this name ring a bell?"

I remembered the name vaguely but couldn't remember the context in which it had been mentioned.

"It turns out," continued Gila, "that this Tony is the father of Valencia's mistress, a young dancer who gave birth to his son. You know this story?"

Now I remembered. It was in the papers that Lisa had left with me.

"Yes, yes. I know exactly what it's all about. What did they say about De la Vega?"

"They said he has, as they phrased it, 'an open account' with Valencia. They said that he feels like Valencia made promises to him and did not keep his word. In other words, he thinks Valencia screwed him. For this reason, he is really angry. They said that someone even heard him say that he wants to teach Valencia 'a lesson he will never forget,' and that if Valencia won't pay him the money freely, he—Tony De la Vega—will make him pay it one way or another."

"Thanks, Gila. That really sounds interesting. I will follow up on it. But that's enough. Go away and forget this ordeal. When I get back, I promise you, I will sit with you and tell you exactly how we nailed the bad guys. Don't worry about anything."

Gila sounded reserved, but still depressed.

"I'm not worried. I know that from this point, I can't help you. I'm sorry that's how it turned out. Bye, and stay in touch."

"Bye, Gila. Have a nice flight," I said, and then hung up.

I finished my coffee, paid and left the café. I was in an excellent mood in spite of being handed a setback in the investigation. Meeka was erased from my memory. The relationship with Lisa painted the world in glowing pastel colors. I walked on clouds all the way to the hotel.

Five minutes later I was entering my room, and I was hit hard in the face the second I walked through the door. This brought me back to the harsh realities of life. I fell to the carpet of my dark room. Sharp pain numbed me and I felt my nose starting to bleed. With tremendous effort, I was able to shake my head and regain my focus. I pushed my upper body off the floor with my hands.

Then I saw him—a short, skinny man running toward me, leaping over me and then running away. I stood up and started running after him, ignoring the rivers of blood still gushing from my nose. The adrenalin rush made the pain vanish, and within seconds, I turned from a winded body on the floor to a hunter determined to catch his prey no matter what.

The poor guy didn't know that he wouldn't be able to escape me. Even though he appeared to be around 50-years-old, he was in excellent physical condition. However, the only thing that mattered now was that I was pissed; I would chase him to hell and back if necessary. I also wanted to know with what instrument he'd used to hit me. It was such a tremendous and effective blow—from a professional standpoint, I mean.

I love the thrill I get from chases. Although I prefer them in a vehicle of some sort—my favorite being a motorcycle—I enjoy foot chases as well. In my first year as a police officer, I ran for over two and a half hours after a drug dealer through the narrow streets of Jaffa and then through Tel Aviv. Rob, on the other hand, was "helping" me from the comfort of our squad car. I lost the suspect a few times, but my intuition put me back on his trail. When I finally caught him, just outside the old bus terminal, it was already daylight. Back at the station, I was equally complimented for my persistence as I was teased for all the energy wasted in the chase.

Rob was my biggest critic on this.

"What are you? You think you're a horse? We have a car, don't we? Why do you need to run like that? If you used your brains a little, you wouldn't have to use your legs as much."

But I didn't pay attention. I loved every second of the chase.

And here I was, running again. My partner in this action, already at the end of the corridor, opened the emergency exit and disappeared.

At the emergency exit, I hesitated for a second. I figured that he was not interested in escaping through another floor and that he would run straight down to the lobby and make his escape through there. I was rushing down the stairs a few steps at a time. My strength returned and I started to jump over the handrails. At first, I only heard his footsteps, and then I caught a glimpse of the back of his sweaty shirt. I reached him the second he tried to open the door to the lobby. I slammed his head against the door and he collapsed.

'Now what?' I asked myself, breathing hard and looking at the sweaty man on the floor. I figured there were three options. The first one, to turn him in to the hotel staff in the lobby, I rejected immediately. It would draw a lot of attention and if Cortez had sent him, my chances of questioning him were zero since Cortez controlled the entire hotel staff.

The second was to wake him up and question him on the spot. But that was not a brilliant idea either. If he shouted or made noise, hotel security would hear him and come to his rescue.

The best solution was to take my time with him. It was likely that he did not speak English, and even if he did, he would probably try to hide it.

So there was the solution: Carry him on my back, unconscious, up to my room on the 10th floor, without anyone noticing.

I had to rest every few minutes. The blood I had lost, the energy I had spent and his weight made the climb very hard. Twice it felt like he was waking up and I had to knock him unconscious again. It took me over 30 minutes to reach the 10th floor. I opened the door to the corridor and was relieved to see it was empty. I ran to my room and threw him on one of the couches.

I took a brown bag from my duffel. It was what I called my First-Aid Kit. It contained useful things like duct tape, scissors, superglue, tacks, nails and nylon rope. That was enough to make sure my new roommate was not going anywhere and would not make any noise.

One of the questions I had wanted to ask him was answered when I discovered on the floor a heavy crystal ashtray stained with my blood. So now I knew what he'd hit me with. Now I could rest a little. I needed to.

When he finally woke up about 20 minutes later and realized his situation, he became terrified. He struggled until he realized that every attempt to free himself, only made the knots tighter.

"Hey, what's up?" I asked him in English with the friendliest smile I could muster under the circumstances. He looked at me as if he were paralyzed. The only moving parts of his body were his eyes, which moved frantically from side to side.

"Do you speak English?" I asked for the record, already knowing the answer. Even if he did know a little, "*Yo no hablo Inglés*" came out in a trembling voice accompanied by an attempt to shake his head.

I knew that even if I were able to find out who sent him, it probably would not be of much use. I was sure he got his orders indirectly and was at the bottom of the food chain. But my curiosity was too great, and I could not release him without learning something about the reason for our encounter.

I decided to call Lisa despite my concerns. I knew how important her job was to her and how her involvement in this investigation could put her at risk.

After calling her, I sent e-mails to Rob and Jody. Just 15 minutes later, I heard the knock on my door.

"Who is it?" I asked and opened the door after verifying that it was Lisa.

When she saw my face, she froze, and I had to pull her into the room.

"I'll explain later. I promise."

I smiled signaling that she could close her mouth, still open with astonishment. Her second shock came when I introduced her to my prisoner. She stared at him with a mixture of disgust and hostility.

"I apologize for calling you, but I need you to translate for me," I told her as I raised the volume on the television set.

"Ask him what he was looking for," I told Lisa.

There was no response. I asked her to repeat the question and again, no response. I smiled at him and punched his face. His cry blended beautifully with the loud noise of the action movie on television.

Lisa froze for a second, shocked, but quickly regained her composure. I asked her to repeat the question and she did with a slight tremble to her voice. I leaned over toward him. He quickly said a few sentences that I did not understand. I looked at Lisa.

"He said he was looking for gold and jewelry, but he swears he didn't take anything. He was here just for a few seconds and then you came in."

My instincts told me he did not pick my suite by coincidence. I leaned toward him and surprised him with a very strong head-butt which snapped his head back. He passed out again. I got a glass of cold water from the bathroom and threw it in his face. It did the job. He woke up immediately.

"Repeat the question and tell him that I have had it with his lies. If he lies again, he will regret it."

My stubbornness proved itself justified. He was sent to

my room to look for documents, photographs, films or anything at all to do with the kidnapping of Carmen Valencia. After a few more 'acts of persuasion,' he told us that Pablo Duran, who does "all kinds of dirty work for the police," as he phrased it, had hired him.

At least some of my curiosity was satisfied. I was sure that if I checked out this Pablo Duran person, I would eventually stumble across mafia types involved in everything that happens in Mexico and beyond.

21.

I tried to organize my thoughts. I had various options and I decided to evaluate them one by one.

Tony De la Vega's threats toward Valencia, which Gila had told me about, were worth following up on. On one hand, it seemed as though they were threats made in the heat of the moment without any real ability to follow through. But maybe someone encouraged him to say these things to keep the attention on De la Vega while the real kidnappers completed their plan.

The information Miguel and Alejandro provided about the relationship between Valencia and his personal trainer, Nate Parker, might prove relevant.

More important, however, was learning more about the relationship between Valencia and Ortega. The probability that the bitter business rivalry led to a criminal act was high.

I remembered an investigation I did two years ago for a 60-year-old New York businessman, a grandfather of five. He had a business empire that included a fleet of oil tankers. He also had a beautiful, former-Playboy-centerfold third wife over 20 years his junior.

One day, an envelope containing photographs of his wife in intimate positions with a young, well-built man was left on his desk for him to find.

His wife denied everything, saying it was not her body in the pictures and that it was some kind of graphics job or photomontage. He initially wanted to divorce her immediately; however, he decided to delay until he learned the truth. That is where I came in. I was supposed to find out if the pictures were real, and if not, find out who was behind all of this.

I was able to locate the male partner starring in the photos—a German porn actor, not a very successful one, who was willing to do almost anything for a payday.

For a few more dollars, he admitted that he had never met the wife.

"I was invited for a photo shoot with another porn actress and that was my part in this. I took the money and left, I had no idea what they planned to do with the photographs and I really didn't care as long as I got paid."

It took me almost a month to find the photographer. He was an Englishman named Larry. I found him in a studio in the Bronx. It took a bit more money to get him to talk, but eventually he did. He admitted creating the montage.

"Where did you get the pictures for the face?" I asked.

"Nowhere. I took them myself," he said with professional pride. "They told me to follow her for a month and take as many photos as possible. The best pictures I took were taken at the gym. She was all sweaty and had this expression women get only when working out or when getting laid. The actress we shot had a very similar figure," he replied. He was not willing to talk about who ordered the work other than say "dangerous people, very dangerous people." I decided not to push him for now.

I returned with this information to my employer.

To my surprise, he said, "That's enough, I can figure the rest of it out by myself." When I questioned what he meant, he continued to explain.

"For the last eighteen months I have been in fierce competition with a Chinese group of businessmen on a bid for transporting oil from the Aegean Sea. They won the contract. I was not as alert and focused as I usually am, and you know why? It is all because I was troubled with this photograph fiasco." He looked gloomy. "I lost because at that critical time, I was out of focus. I don't know how much they paid that guy in the Bronx, but I am sure it was worth every penny. The profits they are going to make are huge. That's the whole story. I am only sorry for being deceived and for doubting my wife's loyalty. But I appreciate the way they operate. As the French say, '*dans la guerre comme dans la guerre*'—'in war like in war,' and business is war.

This memory made me think of Jorge Cortez, "the immediate suspect." It was clear to me that some way or another, his long hand was behind a lot of what was happening. Even if he was not directly involved, it seemed that he might be doing whatever he was doing to benefit from the situation. Only a thorough investigation could unveil exactly what he was up to.

The problem was that I promised Rob, even though half-heartedly, to send all my people home. On top of that, I could not see how I was going to get all the necessary work done in the time that we had. And what if all the people on whom we were gathering information had nothing to do with the crime? I needed to take that into account. What if it was indeed a professional group that had targeted Valencia because he was rich, and none of his people had anything to do with it?

I thought that maybe I should question all of the employees. I later decided against it because of Cortez. If he was involved, he would make sure either he or one of his men would be translating and I would not get any new information even if there was any.

The phone disrupted my concentration.

"Yes?" I answered brusquely.

"Hi, this is Alejandro. I hope I am not disturbing you. Do you have a minute?"

"Yes. Of course I have a minute for you. What happened?"

"I think this will interest you. We followed Cortez. Does the name Tony De la Vega mean anything to you?"

I smiled. "Yes, I know the name. Why?"

"About an hour ago he and Cortez met in a small café outside Mexico City. Half an hour after Cortez left the place, Miguel went in to sniff the place. He befriended De la Vega who told him that he is an 'unofficial in-law' of Valencia and that his daughter had the old millionaire's boy. He also told Miguel that although the old man promised to make him rich, he is not doing it. The son-in-law, Cortez, also hates Valencia and that is the reason, according to De la Vega, he is paying him to tell everyone that he, De la Vega I mean, is going to take a great revenge on Valencia. He actually showed Miguel the money Cortez had given him just a few minutes earlier."

"It kind of matches my information on Cortez, so I am not surprised at all," I told him. I let him know about Gila's release and asked them to stop all activities until I told them otherwise.

"Take the day off and call me at the same time tomorrow. If I need you earlier, I know how to contact you. Most importantly, stay out of trouble."

22.

Valencia, in his usual black three-piece suit, was waiting for me in the backseat of the black Mercedes Benz in front of the Tel Aviv Restaurant at the intersection of Antonio Caso Paries and Insurgents Norte. The driver opened the rear door and I climbed inside.

"Thank you for agreeing to see me on such a short notice," I said as I made myself comfortable in the backseat. "I hope I did not interfere with any special plan you had for tonight. I had to speak to you urgently and..."

"It's all right. I had the feeling that at some point you would want to speak with me in private, outside of my home. You did the right thing."

His expression was very solemn, and he spoke in a quiet tone of voice. With words I did not understand, he addressed the driver who replied, "Si, Señor. Si, Señor," as he opened the door and walked away from the car without looking back.

"Have you ever driven a Mercedes?" he asked me. I understood what he wanted. He acted exactly as I had expected him to. I sat in the driver's seat and started the car.

"I think you will have to direct me where you want to go. Do you have a specific location in mind or is this the 'Mexico City by night' tour?"

"We'll see where life takes us. I am not in a hurry and I have no place to be tonight," he said cryptically.

The decision to have this meeting with Valencia came a few minutes before my scheduled rendezvous with Lisa. Even though I was longing to see her after such an eventful day, I decided to call her and cancel. Business always comes before pleasure.

"Are you bored with me?" she asked in a teasing voice.

"You know I am not," I said. "You know that the thing I want most in the world is to spend the night with you, but I really must have this meeting tonight. Will you call me tomorrow?"

"Of course I will," was her reply. Things can be so simple when you don't want to complicate them. Other women I have been with would have made a big fuss about it. For example, Meeka would not just have been offended; she would have made a scene.

Two weeks into my relationship with her, I was finally able to locate a person I had been hunting for weeks. He had disappeared to avoid being subpoenaed for his divorce trial. I decided to serve the subpoena right away, before he got a chance to go back into hiding. However, she and I had reservations at a fancy restaurant. I called her to say that I would be delayed for about an hour. She was furious and did not want to meet later.

"I have no intention of sitting at home waiting until you finish whatever it is that you are doing. It is not my plan to spend my vacation at home. Do what you think is right, and so will I. You're an adult, Ethan, and you need to get your priorities straight."

Valencia's voice brought me back to the streets of Mexico City, and I was glad. I hated that flashback.

"Make a right turn here. What did you want to discuss with me?" he asked.

"First of all, I want to thank you for what you did to release the woman who works for me. She called an hour ago and…"

"Forget it. I did it at the request of our mutual friend, Rob. I want to believe that this ends the involvement of strangers in this investigation."

I decided to stick to a partial truth.

"She is leaving Mexico tonight on the first plane to Los Angeles. I am sorry, but…"

"This issue is closed, I hope. What else do you want to say?"

I maneuvered the car through the busy traffic, making sure we were not being followed. When the light changed, I turned right on Morales Street. I passed the Christopher Columbus statue and continued south.

"I am trying to locate your bodyguards," I said, looking through the side mirror.

"You're wasting your time. Nobody but the driver knows where I am. I thought it would be better to meet in complete secrecy. That is why I told you over the phone that I would let you know later where and when we would meet. When I desire, I can get past my own people. I have my ways."

"Wonderful!" I said quickly. "There is a plan of action I would like for us to agree upon. It is imperative that no one knows what it is except for us. I also need you to clarify a few things."

"Mr. Eshed, you are the boss. I will do my best to assist you. Please turn right into this parking lot."

I turned into the parking lot of a football stadium. It

was unpaved, and I had to slow down. I came to a stop in front of a gate.

I considered which issue to start with. I had two subjects and neither of them was easy. I decided to start with some questions that were bothering me and for which I had neither the means nor the time to answer by myself.

He noticed my apprehension.

"Ethan, please speak freely. Even if you intend to ask sensitive questions, which I know you do, I want to help. Believe me, I understand a lot more than I am allowing myself to show."

I turned to face him. "First of all, due to the time constraints and my inability to use my people in the investigation, I have no alternative but to ask you these questions directly. What can you tell me about your relationship with Alfonso Ortega?"

"I can tell you what is, by now, common knowledge," he answered. "It was all over the media. We don't have a very loving relationship, as you probably know. We are business rivals in more than one field. You know how it is in business: Sometimes you win and sometimes you lose. I assume you are talking about the "Panorama" affair. It is quite a common business trick. It has been done many times. He was not amused by it, to say the least."

"Do you think Ortega would take revenge on you for what you did in the 'Panorama' deal by putting you through this ordeal?"

Valencia shrugged his shoulders. "Ortega is capable of almost anything, and I have seen him do some dirty and nasty things. But the answer to your question is 'no.' Kidnapping a child is not his style. He would not stoop to such a low level and he would not risk being involved in such a crime. If he were exposed as being involved in such a thing, his career would be over. He is too smart and much too cautious to do it."

"Not even if he throws you out of balance and makes you act under pressure?"

"No. I think not. It is not like him. I know how he thinks. If he were to take revenge, he would want everyone to know it was him in order to restore his pride and reputation. A kidnapper has to hide and that would not serve his interests."

"OK, I accept what you are saying. Now tell me everything about your relationship with Nate Parker."

He kept his cool.

"Nate is my personal trainer. He is fairly new with us compared to my other staff. I think he is doing quite a nice job."

"I am speaking about your nightly visits to his place. Don't you think this kind of arrangement poses a risk to you? This could make you very vulnerable."

"How do you know of our meetings?" he asked abruptly. "I don't think that what I do with my own time is your business or anyone else's." He suddenly realized that it probably had everything to do with my business and asked in a quieter tone, "What exactly are you implying, Ethan?"

"I am just trying to see if we can rule out his involvement in the kidnapping. Has there been any change in his attitude over the last few weeks? Has he made any requests or demands lately? Have you had an argument or something like that?"

"No. Nothing. It seems you are again on the wrong track. Nate is very loyal to me, and if he would have wanted to hurt me, he could easily do it in another way. He could have used the fact that I am using his 'services.' I am doing this because a man of my age, and more importantly, of my *status*, cannot really enjoy life like everyone else. I have weaknesses, and Nate helps me with them and gets paid generously for what he is doing. He has never complained. On the contrary, he seems very happy with our arrangement."

"Are you aware that he was in jail a few times in the U.S.? He was convicted of blackmail, among other things. He was charged, but eventually released for lack of sufficient evidence for participating in a robbery that took place in a diamond-cutting shop."

His astonished expression gave away the answer.

"No, I didn't know that. Are you sure it is the same Nate Parker? That is very interesting. Very interesting, indeed. Are you sure, Ethan?"

I nodded.

"If you want, I can send you a copy of the file. It's pretty thick."

It was obvious that this information had surprised and hurt him deeply. He shook his head in disbelief.

I gave him a few seconds to deal with the blow and then continued, "I'm sorry I have to ask all of these questions, but this is what you hired me to do. What is the nature of your relationship with Antonio or Tony De la Vega?"

He looked tired and weary.

"Señor De la Vega is the father of a good friend of mine."

"Azucar. I know the whole story, but why is he running around telling everyone who will listen that he is going to take revenge on you?"

Valencia squirmed uncomfortably in his seat.

"Look, I don't think...it's a private matter. He says I promised him something. I told him that I would take care of him. He understood it as a promise that I would make him a very rich man. I had something more modest in mind, and mind you, I am paying him a lot more than he has ever had. Regardless, he still dreams of all the millions he thinks he should be getting."

"Do you think he has the personality and the ability to orchestrate such an operation?" I asked.

"The man is a low-life bottom-feeder. He traded in his daughter's body. As an organizer, he is nothing. All he knows is talk and threats. I believe that it is definitely not him."

"I understand that Cortez is taking care of him. How was their meeting tonight?"

I was able to surprise him again. He looked embarrassed. "Cortez met with De la Vega today? It was probably not a planned meeting. Cortez will report to me about it tomorrow morning."

'Yeah, right,' I thought to myself, 'That will be the day.'

Then I said, "I have one last question, with your permission."

Valencia looked worried. "I am starting to fear these questions of yours. They tend to come with unpleasant surprises. I must admit that for the short time you have been in Mexico, you have accomplished a lot."

I didn't respond to his remark.

"There is something that has bothered me from day one, and it has to do with Mr. Cortez."

I paused for a few seconds to give him time to prepare for my question.

"Forgive me for even bringing this up, but I must ask this question: How much do you really trust Mr. Cortez? I know that he is your son-in-law, vice president of your company, your man for special assignments, a partner in some of your businesses, in charge of your security…"

"Ethan, speak freely. Don't move in circles. I'm a big

boy and I have seen things. I am not fragile and I do not collapse easily. What do you want to know about Cortez? Speak up."

"I want you to answer my question. How much do you really trust him?"

He was silent for a while and I didn't pressure him to answer.

"The truth is that I often wonder about him. I have known him for many years and I respect him. Yet, at the same time, I suspect him. He is surely not beyond suspicion if that is the answer you are looking for. Is he involved in the kidnapping? I don't know. It is hard for me to believe he would take such a risk as being involved in something like this. However, as I said earlier, he is not beyond suspicion."

"Excuse me for being hard on you, Mr. Valencia, but if he is not beyond suspicion, can you think of a motive for him to do such an awful thing to you? According to my information, he is not shy of illegal activities when large sums of money are involved."

"Ethan, please tell me what you are getting at."

I took a deep breath and answered frankly, "It is actually very simple. I have no confidence in Cortez. Maybe I'm wrong, but that is my gut feeling. With your permission, I would like to keep him out of our next move. That is, only if you agree."

He did not respond immediately and instead, studied me carefully.

"I am not surprised about your feelings toward my son-in-law. I have never been sure that I could trust him, but I always relied upon my belief that he would gain more by being loyal to me than not. If you think that there is something that he best not be involved in, that is fine by me. Do what you think is right. You have proved your abilities tonight, and I have full confidence in your judgment."

23.

I was following the script I had created for my meeting with Valencia to the letter. My goal was to prove my abilities as a private investigator and to show him how vulnerable he was in many directions. The result I was trying to achieve was to make him realize that I was the only person at this time who was in his corner and could be trusted. His willingness to bypass Cortez was proof of my success.

I weighed my words heavily before speaking. This was the do-or-die moment of this conversation.

"Our next move is designed to force the kidnappers to make direct, face-to-face contact with us, or more explicitly, to have them physically show you that Carmen is alive."

Valencia sat somberly and listened.

"I know," I continued, "that this is a huge risk we are taking, but in our current situation, the only way we can stop them is to expose them. The only rational way to establish the need for such a meeting in the mind of the kidnapper or kidnappers is by doubting that Carmen is alive and well."

I gave him about 30 seconds and then I laid down my punch line.

"If for some reason or other, you decide not to take my advice or if we are not able to convince them to show us the girl, I quit. There is no way I can stay otherwise. The last thing I want is to take your money and not give you results in return."

He was shocked. That was the last thing he expected from me.

"What exactly do you want?" he asked suspiciously. "I do not like ultimatums."

"Mr. Valencia," I repeated, "if for some reason or other this rendezvous between you and the kidnappers does not take place, I prefer to leave. There will be no reason for me to stay. You can give the command back to Cortez. I'm sure that will make him happy."

He didn't like what I told him, that was obvious. He was angry and emotional.

"This is not what I agreed upon with our mutual friend." He raised his voice. "You suddenly make demands that have never been discussed. This is something I cannot promise that will happen. It is not up to me, and you want to leave me alone in this situation."

"The only thing I am asking is for you to insist that there are no further discussions about payment until you see Carmen with your own two eyes. No meeting, no deal. It is as simple as that."

"You know very well that we don't make the rules. *They* do. You should hear the man's tone of voice. He does not converse; he gives orders."

"In the next conversation, you set the terms. You were excellent last time when you made him give you a few more days to arrange the money. You just have to insist. Don't forget that what they are after is your money and that gives you power over them. Use your power. Put your confidence in this strength and stay cool. I know it is a very difficult task, but this is the only way we can achieve both of our goals: the release of Carmen and the capture of the kidnappers," I explained, trying to sound assertive and at the same time, supportive.

"You can even hint that you have no other alternative but to involve your insurance company and they will probably want to conduct an investigation of their own. They know it will delay their payment and complicate things for them. Give them the feeling that it is in their best interest to close things as soon as possible," I added.

I looked at him silently. His face was frozen, refusing to reveal what was going on in his heart and mind. I continued to make my argument.

"You have all the reasons in the world to ask for this meeting. After your terrible experience the last time, you are not willing to proceed before you see Carmen. It is not capricious; it sounds very logical that you would ask for this meeting."

When he started to answer, you could hear the torment in his voice.

"There is no chance that they would agree to this. Why should they risk exposing themselves in such a way? Don't underestimate them; they aren't stupid. They will know it's a trap right away and reject us immediately. They will offer a picture with today's newspaper or something to that effect."

"You will reject all these offers and tell them no meeting, no deal."

"Why do you think that they will agree?"

"Because they will understand from you that this is a deal-breaker. Either you see the girl or the negotiations are over and you are transferring the case to the insurance people. If they feel you are determined to follow through on your resolve, they will be cornered and agree to your terms. You can even tell them that you have already reconciled yourself with the fact that Carmen is gone like Mariana is gone. You will not pay a cent unless you are convinced otherwise. You cannot be fooled twice."

Not too far from where we parked, a group of young people assembled. We could hear them singing in the distance.

They had started a small bonfire. At first, they were standing around the fire gazing hypnotically at the growing flames, then as one, they sat down around it without interrupting their song. This sight took me back to my Haifa boarding school and to Gili, my first big romance.

I was 17 and she was 18. She was tall and very pretty, and most important for a horny 17-year-old, she had monumental breasts. There was not one male in the entire school who did not lust after her, and that included teachers and administrators. I don't know how the older students consummated their fantasies of her, but for us youngsters, she was intangible.

Most students and teachers left to be with their families during spring vacation. Only a few students and faculty stayed in the school. Gili and I were among those few. I don't know what fate had in mind, but of all those left, Gili chose me to be her spring-break companion. She set the rules: the where, the when and the what.

The thing she liked most was going to the beach, lighting a fire and "making love" as she called it. It was the first time I had ever heard that expression. I was a fast learner, however, and quickly understood how to perform the act she was so keen about.

We "did it," as she called it, everywhere—in her room, in my room, in the storage area behind the gymnasium, in the banana plantation behind the school and even once in the girls' bathroom adjacent to her dorm. It was all very exciting, but the nights on the beach by the fire were the most memorable. The combination of the sound of breaking waves, the fire and the lust was the high point of my teenage years.

And then the vacation ended. Everyone came back and that was the end of Gili and I. The first time we spoke after that, she said with a smile, "What happened, happened. And now we each go our own way. Think of it as a nice experience." For me it was the end of the world as I knew it.

I moved my eyes from the fire and looked at Valencia. I knew he understood the logic behind my strategy.

"Believe me, under the circumstances, this is our only chance," I told him. "You have to be strong and stubborn on this issue. It is a gamble we must take, and I truly believe that we have an excellent chance of winning this battle."

"On what do you base this assessment?" he asked with apparent hostility. "The wager here is the life of my daughter."

"What's new about that, Sir?" I inquired calmly. "One way or another, Carmen's life is in danger. There is always the fear that once they get the money, they will get rid of her, like they did with Mariana. You know that, and I know it too. We all know it, and that is the reason you asked me here: to save Carmen and catch the criminals who took her. This is the only way. I don't know another."

I had the feeling that finally, the man in front of me, a man who could buy my entire hometown with the snap of his finger, had stopped resisting me for the naked truth I made him face. I felt a surge of power and continued.

"This was not what we call an 'express kidnapping.'

They didn't immediately blindfold her, so we are pretty sure she would be able to identify them, and they know it.

"I am afraid that they will not be willing to consider our request," said Valencia in a low, pained voice.

"These are desperate people who need the money badly," I said. "They are more than half way to receiving nine million dollars and they will not give it up for the world. They will shout and try to scare us, but when they understand that it is either that or the money, they will cave in. They are too close to their target and they will not jeopardize it."

I faced front with my back to Valencia giving him a chance to relax a little. A young, curious couple tried to peep into our car. A smile was on the girl's face when I looked back at her and she hurried to drag her boyfriend away. A second later they were gone in the darkness.

'So far, so good,' I told myself. There was just one more thing.

"It is crucial that everyone, especially Cortez, knows that it is your idea to ask for this meeting. It must be seen as being your decision and no one else's."

I started the Mercedes and navigated back to the main road. "You must show uncompromising determination. We need to make sure that if the kidnappers somehow get inside information, they will not know that we are doing this as a strategy to expose them. If they catch any word of this meeting and our agreement, they will immediately reject it and we're screwed. Everyone who is part of these negotiations has to think that you have gone out of your mind, and that compromise is not an option. No meeting, no deal. Do you understand me, Mr. Valencia?"

"Yes, I understand. I understand, Ethan. I just hope you know what you are doing."

24.

A sensation of tranquility washed over me. It had been ages since I had felt so relaxed. I let my body unwind and enjoy the warm sun above and the cool grass beneath me. I watched a group of small children close by playing with a ball.

Lisa's head was on my stomach. Her eyes were closed and her face relaxed. My fingers combed through her hair in a gentle motion. Lisa gave in to the pleasure of my touch and the peaceful surroundings.

Only now, lying here totally relaxed, did it occur to me that it had been six years since I had taken a real vacation. Obviously there were those—and Rob was the worst of them—who claimed that my whole life was one long vacation. But he, too, knew very well that an assignment in a foreign city, as beautiful as it might be, was no picnic.

It was true that I always was able to mix business with pleasure. I made a point of it on every out-of-town assignment. I would steal a few hours and sometimes even a full day for myself, but it would be hard to call it a vacation. A real vacation calls for not only a total detachment from your daily schedule and routine, but even more important, a mental detachment that cleanses your head of all your concerns and worries. I had not achieved such a state of relaxation in the last six years.

Even now, in these surroundings, I could not totally put aside the reason for my being in Mexico. Dozens of questions and scenarios ran through my head. While my body was in neutral, my mind was rushing at turbo speed.

"Are you enjoying yourself, Ethan?" I heard Lisa ask.

"Very much," I replied. "I can't remember the last time I enjoyed myself so much."

A few hours earlier, the last thing I would have thought possible was to spend the day doing nothing at all in Chapultepec Park, the oldest park in North America, located just east of Mexico City.

I woke up to a knock at my door. It was exactly 7:00 a.m. Sleepily, I opened the door and Lisa rushed in. She began kissing me passionately as we moved toward the bed, stopping only to take off her clothes. As I laid back she positioned herself on top of me. I fumbled with a condom, but Lisa took it from me, unwrapped it and then slipped it on me using nothing but her moist lips. She totally surprised me on this one. She wasted no time and I felt myself slide deep inside her, pleasure hitting me in waves. I grabbed her hips and thrust even deeper into her with every move she made. Her eyes were shut, her mouth wide open, and her breasts moved in synch with her body. She moved faster and faster, as if nothing could stop her. She was breathing hard and began to cry out.

Then the phone rang. I didn't know whether to pick it up or not. But our concentration had been broken.

"Yes?" I answered, trying to steady my voice.

"Hi, I just wanted to say goodbye before I leave. I hope I didn't wake you up."

Meeka's voice came as a thunderous roar into my consciousness.

"Hey," I said, trying to calm my breathing. My eyes met Lisa's as she got off me and lay down on the bed with her back to me.

Meeka could not possibly know that she had caught me at such an inconvenient time. She sounded surprisingly soft.

"I'm sorry I was such a bitch the last time we spoke. I am sure you have a lot of things on your mind."

'This situation is weird,' I said to myself, grinning at the irony of it all. The fact that the conversation was in Hebrew helped a little. However, I knew Lisa could read me like an open book. I touched her hair with my hand, but she moved away.

"When is your flight leaving?" I asked.

"In about three hours. How are you?"

I sat up, got off the bed, and went to the bathroom. Lisa stayed in bed, following me with her eyes. I smiled at her.

"I'm fine," I told Meeka. "I am really surprised and happy that you called. Our last conversation left me feeling really awful."

"I know and I'm very sorry about that. You know me— there are no filters between my feelings and my mouth. I just wanted to let you know that the past two months with you were incredible. You know that, don't you?"

"Yes, I feel the same way."

"I want you to know that I am very sad to be leaving and I will miss you very much. I don't want to think about how long it will be until I see you. You will call me, right?"

"Yes, for sure," I replied. "Don't forget to call my parents and say 'hi' for me. If you can drop by and have some of my mom's Balkan cooking and the chopped salad my father makes every morning, it would be great." I imagined her sitting with my parents over a Saturday lunch telling tales of America, and I envied her.

"You really are a mind reader! That's one of the first things I plan to do when I get there. Just don't think I'm using them to get to you."

"You don't need them to hook me. I'm already entangled in your net, and you know that you call the shots. It's all up to you."

"I don't want to have this conversation all over again. Unlike you, I'm not an optimist. If you are counting on me to break first, you will be disappointed. Let's leave it the way it is. *Que sera, sera*."

"I will miss you," I said.

"I will miss you too, Ethan."

I sat on the toilet seat staring at the floor. The last thing I was expecting this morning was this phone call from Meeka. This sentimental attitude was not typical of her. What made her act so out of character? Why was she so nice and affectionate for a change? I had no answers and no energy to ponder these questions right now.

I went back to bed and lay by Lisa's side. She stared at me intently. I caressed her face and said, "I'm sorry."

"Was that your girlfriend?"

I was speechless.

"What gave you that idea?" I finally responded.

"Intuition. Your voice became soft. You became emotional. I did not understand the words, but I heard their music. It is very nice that you can express your emotions to people you love."

I hugged her and kissed her lips gently.

"Well this time your intuition was wrong. It was Jody. She had an unpleasant ordeal with her husband and she cried to me over the phone, poor girl."

The phone rang again, and this time it really was Jody.

"Am I disturbing you?" Jody asked.

"No, its fine. Something happened?" I asked, trying to hide the discomfort I felt at having just lied to Lisa.

"There are problems with Jeanne and Alan. She called me hysterically at home a few minutes ago. She asked that you call her immediately."

That didn't sound good, but I tried to stay calm. "Did she tell you what happened?"

"The Dutch police arrested Alan."

"Shit!" I said. That was exactly what I didn't need right now. "How did this happen?"

"He was on surveillance and a neighbor spotted him and called the police. He might be released in a few hours, but you never know."

"I will call Jeanne. Do me a favor, please go to the office and in my bottom drawer on the right side of my desk, there is a stack of business cards. Look for Major Van Lunger. I think he is the commander of the Special Forces with the Amsterdam Police or something like that."

"OK, I'm leaving for the office. I'll be there in 30 minutes. Are you all right?"

"Yes," I answered. "I'm all right."

25.

"What are your plans for today?" Lisa asked suddenly. "Today is Sunday. Nobody should work on Sundays."

The only plan for today was dinner with Valencia and Cortez. "I don't have much of anything planned," I answered as she was heading to the bathroom.

I stayed in bed considering what to do next. I had just had a phone conversation with my Dutch friend, Major Van Lunger, and it had lifted my spirits.

"Let me get back to you on this," he said in his heavy Dutch accent as I explained the situation to him. He didn't even want to know what Alan was doing there.

Later he called to say that there was no need for him to get involved. Alan would be released shortly.

"The police believed that he was just looking for a friend and got lost. They are about to release him. I will make sure nothing goes wrong."

I thanked him and called Jeanne to tell her that she could relax and that everything was under control.

I must admit that the phone conversation with Meeka really rattled me. I had no problem having casual affairs as long as they didn't interfere with an existing serious relationship. But this time it didn't feel right.

The confusion that I had felt when Meeka's call came in surprised and puzzled me. What did it mean? Was my take on relationships wrong? Or maybe it was that one was not a casual affair, but instead, both were serious relationships. Whatever the case, I felt I was unfair to Meeka and especially to Lisa.

"It's such a beautiful day—not too hot. Don't you want to enjoy some of what Mexico has to offer tourists like you?" Lisa asked as she stepped out of the shower.

I must confess that visiting museums and archeological sites seldom moved me. Culture on display behind glass or barriers was not my kind of thing. I prefer to get culture by meeting the local people, going to a café or bar and just starting a conversation. Often some of these new acquaintances became sources or informants, and some of them, even true friends.

On any other day, I would have preferred to spend all the free time I had in bed with Lisa regardless of the weather or tourist attractions. However, Meeka's call threw me off balance, so it was probably a good idea to catch a breath of fresh air.

"I'd love to see what it has to offer. After you, *Señorita, por favor.*"

A few minutes later, we were waiting together with a few hundred locals and tourists for the Number 1 bus that would take us to Chapultepec Park, or "Grasshopper Hill." Just 15 minutes later, we were strolling through the wide-open park, enjoying the shade of some large cypress trees.

It was amazing that so close to this city with its frenzied pace, noise and pollution, there was a spot like this. Actually, the word "spot" does not do justice to this park of over 1,600 acres with an endless variety of activities to offer.

The next five hours were devoted to a sort of "cultural marathon." We visited four of the many museums scattered throughout the park. After the fourth one, I think it was the National History Museum, I told Lisa that I couldn't take another.

"That's it! I'm done. Another museum, and I will have overdosed on culture." I took out my phone and turned the ringer on in protest.

Lisa laughed.

"This is your tour. You decide what we do. How about going to the zoo? They have an amazing dolphin act. What do you say?"

I grabbed her hand and kissed her fingers. Our eyes met.

"You are a little weird today, distant," she said lowering her head. "Are you angry with me?"

I hugged her. "No, I'm concerned with the case. Maybe this is the reason I seem a little distant. Why would I be angry with you? You are the best thing that's happened to me in Mexico."

She held me tight.

"I don't know. After the phone conversation with your secretary this morning, I felt like there was suddenly a barrier between us."

I was lucky she did not see my face. My expression would have given me away. I was stunned by her incredibly accurate intuition. Obviously, she was right. Not knowing what to say, I hugged her.

"What is it with your intuition? This is the second time today that you are off target."

She smiled.

"Maybe. Forget it. Maybe I'm just thinking about stuff. Let's get something to eat. Are you hungry?"

We walked slowly, hand-in-hand, past groups of

tourists, herds armed with their cameras in hand waiting to capture every tree, monument and fountain, and following English-, French-, German- or Japanese-speaking shepherds.

We sat in a small restaurant by a lake. Lisa sat very close to me, the way lovers do. From our corner table, we could see couples rowing boats skillfully between the many ducks and other water birds on the lake. The scenery was entrancing.

"It is very beautiful here," I said. "I am glad you persuaded me to come."

26.

"Ethan, why are you so preoccupied today?" Lisa asked suddenly, changing her position and looking at me. I stroked her hair. In the setting sun, she looked like a pretty teenager.

"From what I understood from you, the meeting with Señor Valencia went just as you wanted it to go. Was there anything you did not tell me?"

I touched her cheeks lightly and smiled. I really loved her gentle features.

"Everything is OK, yet nothing is. Have you ever had that feeling?"

She didn't respond to my smile.

"I still have a feeling that it is not just that. I only met you a few days ago, and it would be presumptuous to say that I know you. But I feel that it is not just the case that is bothering you right now."

How right she was! I was feeling so uncomfortable with myself. The increasingly intense intimacy with Lisa was such an exciting and unique emotional experience for me. That is, until the phone call from Meeka this morning and the destructive self-doubt that followed.

Throughout my years as a private investigator, I have often found temporary companionship for a good time as long as it lasted. I knew that the moment I moved on, the relationship would be added to my memoirs or totally forgotten. The transitory nature of these relationships did not stop me from playing the role of a compassionate lover giving the warmth and attention my partners liked. I always made a point of making it clear to them that they would be better off if they did not take it too seriously. I would tell them to enjoy it while it lasted because a long-term relationship was not on my agenda.

This time, I knew it was different. I felt like a fraud. I was unfair. I had once thought integrity was my strongest virtue. Now I was in doubt. Rob would have said that I was finally growing up.

Had it not been for that unsettling phone call this morning from Meeka, everything would have been wonderful. I liked Lisa very much. My feelings and behavior toward her were sincere. Beyond her amazing beauty, she possessed all the qualities I adore in a woman and a companion. She was pleasant, smart, sensitive, warm and good in bed.

"I don't want you to feel uncomfortable because of me," Lisa said. "I don't know, Ethan, but I have a feeling that you think you are being unfair to me, that you're using me." My poker face didn't work on her. She had read me again.

"Don't take it so seriously. You can relax as far as I'm concerned, really. I am enjoying myself more with you than anyone else. The rest is not important."

I wrapped my arms around her. My phone rang.

"Yes," I answered.

"Hello, this Jorge Cortez. Mr. Eshed, I hope I am not disturbing you."

"Mr. Cortez! What a wonderful surprise. To what do I owe the honor? Is something wrong?"

Cortez sounded wound up. "Yes, something indeed is wrong and I really hope it is not your doing."

"What do you mean?"

"I hope that you are not responsible for Señor Valencia's lunatic decision. He decided not to pay the ransom until he has absolute proof that Carmen is alive. This is crazy! It's a death sentence for the girl! They will never agree to it. They would have to be crazy to accept it. Yet, he insists. He wants to see Carmen with his own eyes. If he doesn't see her, there is no deal."

I enjoyed listening to him lose his temper. I thought it was very smart of Valencia to throw the bait out sooner than we planned. It came across a lot more credible that way. It was more natural that the first person he would share his secret with would be his right-hand man and confidant.

"Are you serious?" I asked trying to sound astonished. "This changes the whole picture entirely."

"That is exactly what I said. With all the respect I have for Señor Valencia and his judgment calls, I think this is a terrible mistake that will lead to a tragic result. I explained to him over and over again that the kidnappers will not only refuse his demands, they will hang up on him and we will lose everything. I asked him what he would do if they disconnected the minute they heard his demands. He had no answer, of course, but he insisted and said that that was the way he was going to handle the situation."

I chose my words carefully. I wanted him to think we were on the same side.

"This definitely is a huge gamble. However, if it works, there are advantages in it for us."

"No, it's too dangerous," he said with conviction.

"This is a terrible mistake that may cost us Carmen's life. You must call him right away and tell him to give up this crazy idea. You need to let him know what the consequences might be for Carmen. Maybe he will pay more attention to what you have to say because you are an outsider."

"Listen, we have a dinner meeting this evening," I said, "the three of us. Let's see how the dice fall. In principal, I agree with you. You realize that for me, the best scenario would be to make the payment, get Carmen and get the hell out of here, the sooner the better."

27.

One of my mottos is, "Believe half of what you see and none of what you hear." Most people believe what they hear and what they see with their own eyes is the absolute truth. Criminal investigation requires a different way of thinking. You must treat everything—sight, sound and actions—as a theory that needs to be proven. Each detail is a piece of a puzzle that needs to be put together meticulously. No one detail gives you the complete picture, and no one fact constitutes proof to substantiate a case.

I learned this firsthand soon after I was recruited to the Drug Unit of the Central Police Division. Based on an intelligence report we had received a few hours earlier, a notorious Tel Aviv drug dealer was planning to visit his wife and newborn baby that night. We were also informed that he would be carrying a decent quantity of drugs with him.

He had been able to elude us many times before and once, when we finally arrested him, he got out within a day or two because of "insufficient evidence." So this new information afforded us a rare opportunity to catch him red-handed.

Our information, obtained from a rival drug lord,

proved itself correct. At 2:30 a.m., he arrived at his wife's home in a Tel Aviv neighborhood.

Unshaven and in faded jeans, he parked his car, took a big, black duffle bag out of his trunk and walked toward the house. We could not have expected things to turn out better for us. There was no doubt what was in the bag. We were elated. We had finally nailed the bastard.

He entered the house calmly. We waited outside in a "pre-war" adrenaline rush.

We waited for the order to storm the house. For some reason, the order was delayed until 4:30 a.m. As we were about to enter the house, we heard shouting and yelling, and the wife screaming, "Help! Help! He is killing us! He is killing us!"

This caught us all by surprise, delaying the break-in by a few seconds, which gave him just the time he needed to leap out of a window with his black bag.

Three detectives chased him while another two detectives went into the house. It was very neglected and dirty, and in the bedroom, we found the wife.

From the information we gathered before the operation, we knew that she had been a social worker who had fallen in love with the dealer when he was in custody. She had become pregnant and they married. Now she was sitting in a dirty armchair, bruised and in tears. She was holding a cute baby girl with big blue eyes, like her mother's.

"Please catch him and lock him up forever," she yelled between bursts of sobbing. "I wish the son of a bitch was dead! I want to live. I need to raise my girl. I want him dead! How could I have ruined my life with that motherfucker?"

She convinced us that her husband thought she was having an affair with one of his friends. In the heat of the argument, he punched her in the eye and threatened to kill her.

She continued to cry, pleading for her husband's capture as we searched the house for more drugs.

"I can't take it any longer! He is a madman! He is killing me! He is killing me! Arrest him! I can't live like this."

It was impossible not to feel sorry for this young woman whose life had gone so terribly wrong. We were very gentle and understanding with her. The baby started crying. She asked us to warm up some milk for her daughter to help her relax and fall asleep.

A few minutes later we got a call over the radio that the dealer had been caught and we were needed as backup at an incident in Jaffa. We left the house.

Once again, the dealer was able to dodge the bullet. The bag he was carrying contained clothes and personal stuff, not a trace of drugs.

It was only a year later, when an associate of his was arrested, that we learned exactly what went down that night.

The drug dealer had noticed our stakeout as he entered the house. He knew that if he headed back to his car, we would catch him with the drugs. So he behaved normally and stepped inside. Immediately, he started staging the scene with his wife's full cooperation. The black eye she had lovingly allowed him to give her added credibility to the show.

And where did the drugs go? A pound of freshly imported, uncut heroin was hidden nicely in the baby's diaper. The same baby we made every effort to comfort. Hence, my motto: Never believe what you hear and only half of what you see.

Now, sitting in Valencia's room, watching his well-planned performance designed for an audience of one—Jorge Cortez—I once again experienced living proof of how true my motto is.

Cortez, this time in a three-piece suit to match his father-in-law's, was shifting uncomfortably in his leather chair. It was evident that he was furious. He believed every word of Valencia's show that had started immediately after we finished dinner and moved to the office to have coffee, smoke cigars and talk business.

This time Valencia chose to sit at his large desk. His posture projected authority. His voice was energetic and his conviction was indisputable. His face wore an expression of severe gravity, and his green eyes took on a unique shade in the dim light. He did not argue and did not try to persuade.

"This is my final decision," he announced firmly. "I do not intend to budge from it. This is about *my* daughter, *my* money and *my* life. I am very sorry if someone does not like my decision. It is his problem, not mine. I have said my final word."

Valencia realized he had sounded a little harsh and impatient.

To put the conversation back on a friendlier note, he added, looking first at me and then at Cortez, "Believe me, Gentlemen, it is not a decision I made arbitrarily. I have thought it over and lost a lot of sleep thinking about it. If I had the confidence that I would get my Carmen back safely, I would easily pay more than nine million dollars. Money is only money, nothing more. But the thought that I would pay all this money so they can throw my daughter's body at my feet—that is something that I can not agree to."

Cortez, sucking hard on his Kent cigarette and unsuccessfully attempting to hide his nervousness, tried for the last time to influence his father-in-law.

"With all due respect, Señor Valencia, I think you are making a terrible mistake. If you start mistrusting these people, then why not take it a step further? They could kill her a minute after you see her or two minutes after they get the money. How can you be sure this will not happen?"

Valencia looked at Cortez with disgust.

"That's why I have you two security experts on my side. You are supposed to know how to deal with these situations. I told you what I want. I want to see Carmen and make sure she is fine. Only then will I transfer the money. Now it is your job to make sure that they keep their end of the bargain. How are you going to do that? I don't know. That is *your* field of expertise."

Cortez gave up. He sat back in his chair looking defeated. That was exactly the moment I had been waiting for.

"Assuming they agree to such a meeting, I believe they will insist that only you, Mr. Valencia, be there," I said in a composed voice. "We also need to think of a scenario in which they will try to kidnap you too, or even hurt you."

Cortez didn't think twice. He quickly tried to exploit the apparent fault in Valencia's plan.

"He's right. It is too dangerous. You must not be exposed to such a risk. You will not know how to handle yourself. One careless move and they might panic and shoot you. I cannot let this happen..."

I interrupted Cortez and said to him, "That is why you must insist that someone else go instead."

Valencia looked at me waiting for a sign as to how he should respond to this turn of events I had initiated. Cortez was facing Valencia, and I nodded to Valencia behind Cortez's back. He understood me immediately.

"I have no problem with that. That is, if you both agree. As long as I know she is well, I will leave the details to you two. You are the professionals and you obviously know what is best for me.

"I still don't think that they will agree to the meeting." Cortez was talking to himself knowing he would not be able to change Valencia's mind. "They've got all the cards. What logical reason would they have to allow us to set conditions?"

Since he saw that Valencia was not even listening, he addressed me.

"Mr. Eshed, with your experience, if you were the kidnapper, would you agree to such terms? Wouldn't you suspect that it is a trap devised to expose you?"

I nodded.

"Of course I would be suspicious. But if I understood that there was no other way to get paid, then I might accept that this was a sincere precautionary step on your side. I might also be convinced that the only reason was indeed to make sure that she was alive before the payment was made."

Cortez looked at me with suspicion.

"And what are we really planning to do?"

"As I understand it, nothing," I answered and looked at Valencia as though seeking his approval. "Everything we do behind their backs contradicting the agreements will put Carmen at risk. We must not confirm any of their suspicions. All we need to do is make sure that Carmen is still alive, arrange the money and make the exchange. Am I right, Mr. Valencia?"

Valencia backed me up.

"Yes. You're absolutely correct. I don't want any action, or car chases or anything like that. All I want is for someone to make sure she is alive, pay the ransom and get the girl. That is all—nothing more, nothing less."

28.

It was almost midnight when I arrived back at El Presidente. I turned on the light and as usual, I checked to see if I had had any uninvited visitors. The two 'souvenirs' I'd left in strategic places were still where I had placed them, and I was content.

I took off my suit and headed straight to the shower. I realized that in spite of the intense day, I was not tired. On the contrary, I was more alert than ever.

My first call was to Jeanne.

"Everything is all right," she announced. "I hope we didn't cause you too much trouble. It was very unpleasant, but you know how it is—stuff happens."

"The most important thing is that Alan is OK," I said. It was an instinct from my military-commander days. The well being of your soldiers is always first priority.

"He is fine. It ended a lot faster than we thought it would. They believed his story about being a tourist and getting lost and all that."

"Great. What's with the case?"

"Our original plan was to serve him the day after tomorrow. Now, because of what happened, I think that to be on the safe side, maybe we should delay it for a few days. What do you think?"

It made sense to me.

"It's up to you. If you think that it's better to wait then do it, just make sure your bird doesn't fly the coop."

"Sure. Alan is checking on him as we speak."

The second phone call was to Ricardo. I got a hold of him in a little pub, not far from the hotel where he was staying.

"It's good to hear from you, Man. I was starting to get bored here," he said.

"I need you to get in touch with Alejandro and Miguel. Tell them to be alert. I will need all of you pretty soon. Do you still have the van?"

"Yes. It's in an underground parking garage with all the equipment. I didn't want to move it around, you know."

"I need you to have it ready immediately. Wait for my call. Once I call, there won't be any time. So do everything now. Did you have a chance to speak to Gila?"

"Yeah, she's fine. She said to tell you she is very sorry for what happened."

I put on jeans and a black T-shirt and went down to the lobby. One of my personal favorites, Frank Sinatra's song, "My Way," was playing. Despite the late hour, the place was packed. I made my way to the bar, making sure that there were no suspicious characters in the crowd.

I was seated at the far corner of the bar when I noticed the Palestinian barman, the same guy who was on duty my first night at the hotel. He smiled at me like a long lost friend.

"How are you this evening, Sir?" he asked.

"Fine, thanks. And you, Muhammad?"

"As you can see, things are very busy tonight. Do you want anything special or are you sticking to your regular?"

"The regular, please."

He went to make my drink and I made use of the time by scanning the room. It was filled with cigarette smoke. Two women were dancing together sensually, attracting the curiosity and attention of a group of young spectators.

In another corner, a bunch of middle-aged men who appeared to be American tourists, sat silently, gazing emptily at the late-night activities. They were apparently drunk and looked extremely out of place. Another group of young men and women were crowded around a small round table, talking and laughing. Every once in a while, loud yells of "*¡Orale!*" from the group eclipsed Frankie's "Strangers in the Night" which was now playing.

"Here's your whisky, Sir. I hope you have a nice night. If you need anything, just let me know."

"Thank you very much," I replied.

A good-looking woman with blue eyes and short blond hair sat at the bar not too far away from me. I stared at her with obvious pleasure. She was probably in her mid-40s, but still looked great. For a split second, our eyes met and she smiled an inviting smile. And then I felt a forceful slap on my shoulder.

"I can't believe it! You are the last person on Earth that I would expect to meet here."

"Zion Cohen!" I exclaimed in a tone that sounded like a policeman meeting his arch-nemesis. My surprise was as great as his.

The small man in a thousand-dollar suit stood in front of me, grinning. I was glued to my seat, having a hard time believing that it was really him. Until three seconds ago, I could have sworn that this man, who dragged me through one of the weirdest cases of my career, was no longer among the living.

"What a small fuckin' world, eh, Ethan?" He said in

Hebrew. "I wanted to call you like a million times, but I thought you were still angry with me, so I didn't."

I was angry with him, sure. But even more, I was angry with myself.

We had first met when he was a small-time hood who dealt drugs in the southern, poverty-stricken neighborhoods of Tel Aviv. After a long period of surveillance, we caught him and some of his gang members. During the interrogation, my colleagues grew to like him. He had a smooth tongue and he was funny. They cracked up when he told them jokes and they loved the proverbs he used all the time, relevant or not. I didn't buy into his act and I did not bother to conceal my resentment.

He decided that I was prejudiced and that I was looking to "nail him," as he phrased it. When he was sentenced to three years in jail, he saw me as the person responsible and threatened that I would "pay dearly" for every day he spent behind bars.

The next time I met him, many years later, was in Los Angeles. I used to frequent an Israeli-Lebanese restaurant close to my home. I enjoyed talking to fellow Israelis over delicious shawarma sandwiches.

One day, I found myself sharing a table with a small-framed, bearded man. He was staring at me, but I ignored him. I was too busy devouring my sandwich.

"Excuse me," he finally addressed me. "By chance, is your name Ethan?"

Only then did I recognize him.

"Yes, Cohen, it's me. It has been a long time since we sat on opposite sides of the same table. What brings you to the City of Angels?"

We conversed for a few minutes like old pals reuniting. I have neither ethical nor moral problems making personal contact with convicted felons. In my line of work, you never know when such connections might come handy. This conversation was not an exception.

He told me that a year earlier, he had a "professional disagreement" with his friends/partners in the gang and had to "release the pressure," as he phrased it. He got together with his elder brother, who was already operating in the US, and he started up with his previous occupation.

I didn't ask and I didn't want to know. Since I was late for a meeting, I gave him my business card and said goodbye.

"If you ever need anything, you're welcome to give me a call."

I thought that giving him a business card and telling him he could call was just a formality—but with him, it was one surprise after another.

Three months later, while I was sitting in my office reading a professional article, Jody called me on the intercom.

"You have a guest. He doesn't have an appointment, but he said he is your friend from Israel."

"I have a deal for you," he said as I showed him around the office. "We could make a lot of money together if we did it wisely. Are you interested?"

"Talk to me," I answered without emotion.

"My brother and I were working with a local gang, Columbians, specializing in smuggling valuable antiques from South America. They hide them in a fuel truck that has a double lining. Each shipment is worth 30 to 40 million dollars."

It seemed, however, that the Cohen brothers had run into a conflict, and the Columbians were trying to cut them out of the business.

"I know," he continued, "that the law in the U.S. says that if you assist the authorities in catching antique smugglers, you get 15 to 20 percent of the recovered value. Do the math; we are talking about six million divided by two. That's three million each. What do you say?"

I was not quick to show enthusiasm.

"Why do you need me? You have all the information and all you need to do is contact the FBI and make a deal with them. I am totally redundant here." Obviously, I knew that if that were the case, he would not have been here, but I wanted him to explain it to me.

He smiled.

"They will treat it differently if it comes from you rather than from me. They know and trust you. If I go to them, they will start asking questions—some of them, the kind I don't really want to answer. They will place conditions and limitations, and more important, if I go personally, the word will probably reach the Columbians and you know how they treat people who go to the police. Whatever you decide to do, you must promise that no one will know of my proposition."

Rob confirmed that indeed there is a reward for helping recover stolen antiques.

"I understand that your operation is not enough. Now you are doing jobs on the side," he teased me.

I told him that my interest in this was purely academic, but actually, I had started to seriously consider it. Eventually, I called my friend Steve Hamilton who had recently been appointed to the post of Commander of the Special Forces Los Angeles Unit of the FBI. I had met him when I helped an owner of 12 nightclubs shake off a gang that demanded he pay 'protection fees,' or they would torch the clubs. My assignment was to gather evidence, document the gang's activities and give the information to the police without the involvement of the club owner. So I did, and as a bonus, I got to know Steve who became a close friend.

"It sounds very interesting," he said when I described the situation to him without revealing my source. "If we catch them, you will indeed receive a nice reward. It is important you are aware of that. In any case, I would be glad to cooperate with you on this one."

I told Cohen about my conversation with Hamilton and he said he would let me know when the merchandise was scheduled to cross the border, as well as the description of the trucks.

Four days later, he called and said that the shipment in four trucks would be leaving Mexico in two days. I notified Steve, who called me later that day to inform me that a special task force of 30 FBI agents would be ready to intercept the cargo.

That morning, I sat in the forward command center with Steve and some other FBI officers waiting for information. At 10:30 a.m., he called.

"The trucks crossed the border and they are on the 5 Freeway headed toward Los Angeles," he said.

The task force was put into position in the southern entrance to Los Angeles. I had already started dreaming about buying my parents a new house and myself, a rare Harley-Davidson I had seen a few years back at a collector's house.

And then Cohen called and I went outside to take the call in private.

"We have a problem." He was short of breath. "They are suspicious and they are sure we ratted them to the police. They already paid a visit to my brother and beat the shit out of him. I'm sure they are on their way here."

"Where are you now?"

"I'm home. If I run, they will know their suspicions are

true and that's the end of the Cohen family. It would be better to stay here and try to convince them we had nothing to do with it."

What should I do? I didn't know if the trucks had been alerted and ordered to take a different route or perhaps just return to Mexico. I could have told the FBI to stop every fuel truck coming into Los Angeles, but that wouldn't have been effective. Plus, it was obvious that if they did so, it would be a death warrant for my source. Just the irregular check would point a finger at him and the price for that was death.

"What's happening, Ethan?" Steve asked when I returned inside the command center.

"There is no shipment," I said, truly embarrassed. "I was notified that the trucks changed course at Laguna Niguel and crossed back into Mexico. It looks as though somehow our plans were leaked out. I don't know yet what went down."

The room became silent. Some of the agents stared at me with loathing. Steve cussed graphically. Then he pulled himself together and patted me on the back.

"Stuff happens. It is not very pleasant, but in our profession, things like that happen. Maybe next time."

All my attempts to locate Cohen were unsuccessful. His voice on the answering machine in broken English and a heavy accent saying, "I am not available. Leave a message. I call back," was all that was left of Zion Cohen.

For a few months, I tried to find out what had happened to him. All I heard were rumors. They said the Columbians whacked him, and one person I met even swore to me that he had seen the execution. They said he had been shot and buried at a construction site. A while later, I saw his brother who told me he was in Israel. I looked for him there—nada. It looked like the earth had swallowed up Zion Cohen.

And here he was, right in front of me. He had not changed much. The only changes I could see were his hairstyle—he was a little balder—and a scar.

"You don't know how much I appreciate that you made them back off. I owe you my life," Cohen gushed.

I asked him where he had been since then.

"I was sure they'd finished you. I even know where you are buried."

He laughed.

"I am so happy to see you, Ethan. I have thought about you many times since then. Doing what you did, Man, you're bigger than life itself."

In his funny and picturesque language, he told me what happened to him after our last phone conversation.

A few minutes after we spoke, four Columbians arrived at his place. He tried to convince them that their suspicions were baseless, obviously without much success. They hit him hard.

"You see?" he asked, pointing to the scar on his face. "This is why I'm wearing this stupid hairdo. This is a souvenir from that day. They also broke both my legs and four fingers. And the teeth? They're brand-new, thanks to my Columbian friends. At one point, I said, 'Just kill me and be done with it!' But they had so much fun with me alive, why ruin it? Then they got a call that the merchandise was safe. So they left, but not before telling me to leave town and kicking me again in the...you know where."

The only reason he was alive today was because the trucks were not searched, and that was my doing!

"Can I buy you a drink?" he asked.

"No, thanks. I was about to go back to my room. I have had a very busy day and tomorrow will not be any easier."

"I insist. This is the least I can do after what you did for me. I don't know if I would have done for you what you did for me."

I was absolutely sure he wouldn't have done it. He would sell his mother for a lot less.

I nodded to the bartender and signed the tab.

"I am glad to see that you are alive, and good luck with whatever it is you are doing here. Take care of yourself, Cohen." I left the bar without looking back.

I have made many mistakes in my life and I make every effort not to repeat the same mistake twice.

29.

Lisa insisted, "I really don't understand why you don't let me help you. The more I think about it, the more I am sure that I am the best person for this job. Ethan, please...let me do it."

"No, Lisa. I am not willing to let you participate in an operation when we don't know how it will end. You are already taking a huge risk just by being seen with me. I don't want to make things worse. I could never forgive myself if something happened to you out there. These are people who do not hesitate to kill."

She was on her knees on the floor in front of the big armchair in which I was sitting. She put her hands on my knees and looked up at me with that beautiful face.

"Convince me that I am not the most suitable person for this. Who can you trust more here in Mexico City? Because I am a woman, the kidnappers will not feel threatened by me. What could be better than that?"

What she said made a lot of sense. She had all the qualities needed to stand in for Valencia, assuming the kidnappers agreed to the meeting. I could not expose my men, Alejandro, Miguel or Ricardo. I needed them to locate and capture the kidnappers after they have left the meeting place. Obviously, I could not rely on Cortez and his people. I had no reason to trust any of his direct employees. There were too many questions about his conduct throughout this ordeal, including his objection to Valencia's condition to see Carmen before paying the ransom. Relying on Cortez might jeopardize the success of the mission.

I would have loved to do it myself. That would be the ideal solution. I could use the situation to take in details that an untrained eye would not notice. Usually, these little things alone can make the difference between success and failure. Unfortunately, I was automatically disqualified because I did not speak Spanish. Communicating with Carmen and her kidnappers was a crucial part of the meeting. For the same reason, I ruled out asking Rob to come, although with his experience and easygoing demeanor, he would be ideal for this assignment.

I thought about using Daphne, an Israeli girl living in Mexico City, but discretion wasn't her best attribute. I didn't trust her to keep her big mouth shut. A few wrong words to the wrong people could ruin everything.

Eventually, I decided to call Camilla, and do it immediately following the phone conversation between Valencia and the kidnappers.

Camilla was a very close friend. She was born in Mexico, and I knew I could count on her to do it.

She was more or less my age, and of medium height with long black hair and a full figure. When I met her a short while after moving to Los Angeles, she was working with a foundation advocating the rights of Mexican immigrants. Later, due to her resourcefulness and enthusiasm, she became the chair of the foundation and one of the most influential figures in the Mexican community of Los Angeles.

At the time, we were also next-door neighbors in an apartment building in West L.A. Both of us were new to this sometimes-intimidating town, and not knowing many people drew us together. We spent many nights together, talking and drinking. Our physical relationship was limited to a goodbye kiss on the cheek. Even after she'd moved from the building, we remained in close contact.

Camilla could easily be the contact person. I was sure she would love to help me and at the same time, visit her family here.

And now Lisa was offering herself for the job. I was surprised by the offer. Yet, I was also relieved. I was sure that after the events of yesterday morning, when she figured that my head and maybe even my heart were with someone else, she would back out of our relationship. I feared the worst, and I was glad to learn that maybe I overreacted.

I told her about the dinner at Valencia's place and the demand he made to meet the kidnappers. I also told her about my plan to bring Camilla in.

"I will do it," she said. "Why would you want to bring someone from over there when I can do it? What makes her more qualified than I?"

If things were different, I would have probably accepted her offer gladly. In the past, I did not hesitate to use—and that is the only term to describe it—my female partners. Never before had my conscience interfered in such decisions. As far as I was concerned, the end justified the means.

Not this time. Not with Lisa. Even with all the love and affection I felt for Meeka, Lisa was not just another fling. I had to admit that even in the short amount of time we had known each other, my feelings toward her were deeper than I had realized and more than I'd ever intended them to be. You don't use a loved one.

"I really don't understand why you don't want to let me help you," she said as her hands started to slowly make their way to my waist. "I think I have proven how attached I am to you. After everything we have shared these last few days, you still do not have faith in me? You still think someone sent me to spy on you?"

"Of course I trust you. I would trust you to lead me blindfolded over a narrow bridge with alligators on one side and sharks on the other. The thing is…"

I hesitated and my voice became softer.

"The thing is, you are too dear to me. Lisa, this is dangerous, very dangerous. I don't want you involved because I don't want you hurt, not now and not ever. A week from now, I will pack my bags and leave. I don't want someone to settle the score with you because of things that I have done."

"I am not afraid, Ethan," she said as she stood over me. She sat on my lap and pulled my face toward hers.

"I proved to you that I am not scared. If I were, then I would not be here now, would I? If my father saw us now, the only dilemma he would have is who he would kill first."

I wrapped my arms around her and pulled her to me.

"It's wonderful you want to help, but you are way too important to me. To you it might look like a small, fun adventure, but believe me, it's not. We are dealing with madmen who might act very unpredictably and not hesitate to kill. The last thing I want is to see you hurt. You are very dear to me."

She kissed me tenderly.

"Thank you, Ethan. It was very important to hear you say that and I truly believe that you are sincere, probably more than you planned to be or want to be. However, I really want you to reconsider my request. I have not asked you for many things, right? I ask you to let me do this. Please, please, please."

She was so cute when she said that, and it made me want to shut her up with a big kiss. Her shiny green eyes gazed at me, teasing and inviting.

Since I did not move, she jumped to her feet. The magical moment was over. Now she was nice, but practical.

"Come walk with me a little. I still want to get to the library. I haven't finished my paper yet. Do you feel like it, or do you want to stay here all day and do nothing?"

30.

"El Presidente Hotel, Señor?"

"Yes, please."

I sat comfortably in the backseat of the luxurious limousine and opened the window. I needed a breath of fresh air to relax and to think about the events of the last hour.

At first, everything went as we had planned. At the set hour, the golden phone on Valencia's desk rang. With a severe expression on his face, Valencia let it ring a couple of times before answering it.

I appreciated his calm posture even in the toughest of times. Even though I did not understand what he was saying, it was evident that he was in control of himself and the conversation. He did not raise his voice and spoke with a calm firmness, exactly as I instructed him to do.

"Make them feel that you are one-hundred-percent firm with your decision and that you will not budge from it no matter what their response is. Let them know that if you do not see Carmen, there is no deal."

The phone conversation lasted for three or four minutes. Although I did not understand the words, I tried to understand everything through his expressions. It was only toward the end of the conversation that he raised his voice slightly.

The room became silent. Valencia stayed in his chair.

"It's not going to work," I heard Cortez saying from the back of the room. "I told you. Only fools would agree to these terms."

A sense of disappointment overcame me. I stood up, my eyes fixed on Valencia, trying to catch his eye.

"Mr. Valencia, would you please tell me what they said?"

He raised his head. A cloud of sadness darkened his face. It was obvious that answering my question was very hard for him. "He…he said that they…that they need time to think about it. He was very nervous and repeatedly said that I am playing with my daughter's life…that I am playing with fire."

"What did he mean by saying that they need to think about it? How much time did he say they would need?"

Señor Valencia shrugged.

"He didn't say. He only said that they needed to think about it, and that I am playing with fire."

"Did he say when they would get back to you?"

"No," he replied. "I pray I did the right thing. He asked why I was not using my insurance."

Cortez's voice was full of appreciation for the kidnappers.

"They are no fools. You can say many bad things about them, but they are not stupid. I am afraid this was a mistake. I just hope it is not too late."

I didn't let him finish the sentence.

"I don't understand why you are so quick to despair. If I understand correctly, and please correct me if I'm wrong, he did not categorically reject the idea. All he asked for was some time to think it over. In my book, that means that he understood your message. Obviously, he didn't like it, and we knew that he would try to make you change your mind by threatening and applying pressure, but the bottom line is that he got the message."

The two men listened to me in silence. I used the center stage I was given to encourage Valencia, who was still very solemn.

"We are not yet where we want to be; however, it is way too early to give up," I said in a confident tone.

"Whoever spoke with you is probably only a messenger, not the decision-maker. That was why he had to say that he would get back to you. He needed to consult and get approval from the leader. Mr. Valencia, who knows better than you that part of the game of negotiations is creating real and artificial times of tension and crisis? It is part of the game, and this delay needs to be taken as such. Try to remember: How exactly did he respond when you said that you would not pay the ransom without seeing Carmen?"

"He was angry, of course. He repeated the phrase, 'You are playing with fire.' I had a feeling that he knew why I was demanding to see her, but I can't be sure of that…"

Cortez interrupted him.

"What I suggest is that when they call back, and only God knows when that is going to happen, you consider, according to the way they respond, withdrawing your ultimatum. With all due respect, I think you pulled their rope a little too tightly, so to speak. I am sure that you will agree with me if I say that it is more important to have Carmen back than it is to catch these criminals."

Valencia shot him an annoyed look. Cortez froze in the middle of his sentence.

In a trembling voice, he muttered, "At least this is what I think. The decision is yours."

Señor Valencia cut him off firmly.

"The decision is indeed mine and I have made up my mind. No meeting, no deal." In a surprisingly swift move, he stood in front of Cortez. "The ultimatum stands. I am not backing off. We stick with this line all the way. Maybe I am gambling on Carmen's life, but I will not let them deceive me again."

Cortez tried to say something, but Valencia hushed him with a wave of his hand.

"I respect both of your professional opinions, but this is my decision to make and mine alone. If either of you cannot accept it, you are welcome to remove yourself from this case."

The room became silent again. Cortez was pale as a ghost.

Then Valencia asked me, "Assuming they will agree to my conditions and a meeting will take place, who will be the one who will go? I understand that you think it is too dangerous for *me* to go. So who will it be?"

"I agree with Mr. Cortez that you should not go. I would have preferred to be the one, but since I don't speak the language, it is not a good idea."

Cortez was quick to suggest that one of his men go.

"It is important that whoever goes is professional. I will assign…"

"That is exactly what I am afraid of," I said. "A professional, even if he appears calm, will cause tension. I don't want to underestimate the kidnappers' professionalism. They have already shown that they are smart enough to use unregistered and untraceable cell phones and other high-end equipment."

"So what do you suggest?" asked Valencia.

"First of all," I replied, "I would prefer it to be a woman. A woman won't cause them to be as apprehensive. She needs to look nice and maybe be skilled in martial arts. She needs to know Spanish and be acceptable to you, Mr. Valencia."

When I glanced at Cortez, he was looking at me with such hatred it was palpable.

"I don't know why we can't send an experienced person who knows how to act in such situations. I don't believe they will really care who the person coming on our behalf is if they agree to our requirements."

I smiled at him with the friendliest smile in my arsenal.

"Mr. Cortez, on any other occasion, I would absolutely agree with you. However, this case is different in the sense that they are very suspicious already. We need to make sure they don't get jumpy. As you said earlier, they are probably paranoid enough to think we are plotting to catch them. This is why I think that the person going on our behalf should be one who can convey the most confidence possible and be the least threatening. They will designate the meeting location to their advantage, and at the first sign of trouble, all hell will break loose. Don't forget that once the meeting takes place, they have nothing more to lose.

Valencia and Cortez concentrated on what I was saying. They guessed that I already had a candidate and waited for me to reveal her identity.

"I want to use a friend of mine," I said. "She was born in Mexico, and naturally, her Spanish is fluent. She has done some work for me in the past, so she has some background. She is very reliable and loyal, and I am sure she will be very good."

Cortez's response did not surprise me.

"With all due respect, Mr. Eshed, while I understand

your apprehension about sending a man to the meeting, I still think it is wrong to use amateurs. In my security detail there are six women, all very experienced, and each one of them glad to risk their lives for Señor Valencia."

"Mr. Cortez, I would rather not use anyone from your team. I have nothing personal against you or any of your people, but I would rather have one of my own as the person who goes to the meeting."

Cortez looked astonished as he looked from me to Valencia and back again.

"I thought we are all on the same side," he said angrily, almost shouting. He then looked back at his father-in-law. "The decision is yours, Señor, however, it is impossible for me to understand why you should use inexperienced people for such a crucial assignment."

Valencia stood up.

"Since this whole discussion is theoretical, at least until they call back and confirm the meeting, I will not make a decision right now. I am sorry. I am very tired. With your permission, I would like to go to my room and rest. We will continue this discussion tomorrow."

"And what if they call tonight?" insisted Cortez. "I think this is a very important decision that can't be postponed. We also have to decide what to do if they do not accept our demands."

Valencia lost his patience with Cortez.

"I told you already that I have no intention of starting a manhunt. I don't want surveillance, arrests or anything like that. All I want is Carmen—alive. The rest is of no interest to me. I think we've covered that more than once."

Now, in the limousine, I went over the meeting. The way Cortez acted and responded to my suggestions made my old suspicions of him resurface. I was reminded of what Rob says: "If it looks like a duck, walks like a duck and quacks like a duck, it's probably a duck." So why did I not trust him?

Maybe it was because Señor Valencia had been holding this duck close to him for many years now and even if it was not with complete trust and confidence, Cortez was still a key player in his business and life.

His objection to one of my people being the representative for the meeting with the kidnappers was clear and could easily suggest that he had an ulterior motive. He was Valencia's right-hand man and son-in-law, but I had seen it happen before where the man closest to you is the one causing you the most harm.

I witnessed it firsthand when I conducted an investigation for a young woman, a daughter of one of the richest families in Texas.

She suspected that a 'mysterious hand' was making sure that her mother would not recover from her illness.

"Someone here is trying to kill her. We have got to save her," she pleaded desperately.

I learned from the daughter that her 60-year-old mother had been suffering for a few months from an unexplained series of severe illnesses. Most of her days were spent in bed, medicated with the various drugs her doctors prescribed.

I also learned that the mother had a personal nurse who lived on the family's big ranch. The best and most expensive specialists were treating her, but for whatever reason, her condition was worsening. The test results were inconclusive. However, the doctors did not rule out that something or someone was poisoning her.

The mother was not an easy person to be with. I learned that before her illness, she was demanding and very hard on the ranch staff. When I asked the daughter if the family suspected anyone, she named a few of the employees who had been treated harshly by her mother, focusing on those who had access to her private quarters.

"And what about your father?"

She laughed.

"Are you serious? My father? Her husband? He is not only the person closest to her; he also takes care of her with complete devotion. He has not spared any expense to get her the best treatment available. He prays every day for her recovery."

We decided to bring in an undercover person to work on the ranch. Cybil was perfect for the job. I recruited her five months earlier for a job and she had proven herself very useful on a variety of assignments. She was a pleasant person and a nurse by profession. She took over as the mother's private nurse in place of the regular nurse. She was there for two months and had nothing irregular to report. The woman's condition continued to deteriorate. I asked Cybil about the father.

"He is a wonderful person," she said warmly. "He is all soul. He cares so much for her—is so devoted. He would do anything for her."

Out of desperation, I planted two miniature cameras in the room, one in the bathroom and one above the mother's bed. The cameras were easily operated by remote control. I taught Cybil how to turn on the cameras when she left the room and turn them off when she came back.

After a week, the mystery was solved. The recordings showed conclusively that the woman was being poisoned by her husband. He used the moments when the nurse was out of the room to slip a small dose of poison, which he kept in a tiny bottle in his pocket, into his wife's water glass.

Before notifying the daughter, I wanted to find out why he was doing it. It took just two days of surveillance to figure it out. The devoted father and loving husband was having an affair with a young woman he met almost every day.

The daughter's shock was understandable as I revealed my findings. She had a very hard time believing that her father, the man she loved so much, was the one trying to murder her mother, his wife. These things can happen even in the best of families. Was it happening in Señor Valencia's family right now?

"El Presidente Hotel. Have a good night, Señor."

31.

It was half past two in the morning when my cell phone started ringing. I barely heard it in the surrounding noise of the pub.

"Yes?" I answered quickly, almost shouting into the tiny device, trying to speak over the music and conversations.

"I am sorry about the hour, but I had to speak with you. A few minutes ago, he called. Are you with me, Mr. Eshed?"

I recognized Valencia's voice immediately. I let go of Lisa's hand and started making my way outside stumbling over chairs, tables and people.

"Yes, Mr. Valencia, I understand that they have contacted you."

Lisa stayed behind and I felt her eyes staring at my back as I made my way out to the street. I hoped that Valencia wasn't hearing the background noises. The last thing I wanted him to think was that I was partying while he was trying to keep calm at this tense and anxious time.

"He called a few moments ago. They accepted. He said they would call in the morning to tell us when and where the meeting will take place. We need to get ready."

Loud laughter coming from a group of young people prevented me from hearing his last words.

I reached the door and almost ran into two girls who were standing and whispering to each other.

"What exactly did the man say?" I asked while surveying the street.

His voice remained tense.

"All he said was that they will call to tell us the details and that I should have the money ready for them. Have you decided yet who is going to meet them? We have to make some decisions quickly."

Yes, I needed to make a decision right away. Bringing Camilla was now out of the question. It would take too much time, at least a day or two for her to get here. We couldn't ask the kidnappers for another delay now that they had agreed to our terms. They would think that we were playing with them, and there was no telling how they would respond.

"Yes, I have someone who will do it. She is local and she is exactly the type of person we need. I trust her explicitly. I want you to meet her and I hope you will be as impressed as I am."

"No problem."

"All right, Mr. Valencia. I suggest that you get some rest now. I will be at your home at 7 a.m. with her if that's OK. If it's too early, we can do it later."

"No, that's fine. I will see you then."

When I turned back toward the pub, Lisa was at the door. She looked worried.

"Did anything happen?" she asked as she walked over to me.

I didn't answer. I looked at her. She was beautiful. A young stud in black leather pants passed by and made some comment. She ignored him.

"What happened, Ethan?" I reached for her and hugged her. She put her head on my chest and held my waist. I loved smelling her hair.

I reevaluated my decision of just a few seconds ago to have Lisa meet the kidnappers and verify Carmen's well-being.

I had no other option. With the new time constraints, Lisa was the only alternative. Earlier that day, I had refused to allow her to be involved even though she begged me to let her do it. Our connection had become a bond of love and the thought of exposing her to danger was unacceptable to me.

If everything went according to plan, there would be no reason that she would be harmed during the meeting. The meeting would last only a few moments and there would be no reason for a confrontation to develop.

The meeting was not the problem. What I really worried about was the future. I knew that if I captured some of the gang, the others would most likely retaliate. Valencia, his family and his employees would be protected. I would not be around. The only person involved that would be exposed to their revenge would be Lisa. She would be an easy target for any assassin. I couldn't let that happen.

Also, I was ashamed to admit that part of me still did not trust Lisa. Doubts that I had when I first met her still lingered. My emotions and my professional experience were still battling it out.

It was one thing to have a relationship with a beautiful girl with whom I'd crossed paths. But to entrust her with the most crucial part of an investigation I'd been hired to conduct was something different.

I knew I was crossing a personal red line. I was putting

faith in emotion and intuition over reason. An inner voice told me to trust her totally—do or die.

I held her tightly and finally whispered in her ear, "I need your help." She wanted to look at my face, but I prevented her from doing so by putting my hand on her head and caressing her hair.

"I hope that I am doing the right thing and that neither of us will regret it."

"You will not regret it, Ethan," I heard her whisper. "I promise you. You will not regret it."

32.

Lisa captured Valencia's heart the minute he laid eyes on her. I didn't understand a word they were saying, but the wide smile on the distinguished man's face said it all. An instant rapport had developed between the two. I was relieved.

Lisa looked prettier than ever. She wore a pair of tight blue jeans that complimented her figure and a white shirt that contrasted wonderfully with her black hair. Blue high-heeled sandals completed her outfit. She was stunning.

I went out to the balcony to allow them some privacy. There, I called Ricardo who answered immediately.

"What's up?" I asked.

"We're waiting for instructions," was his answer. "I have prepared everything: the van, the equipment, everything. I am in touch with Alejandro and Miguel. They are waiting for my signal. Do you know the schedules, the routes and all the rest?"

"Nothing yet," I said pacing back and forth. "I hope that in an hour or two I'll have some answers. In the meantime, be ready and stay in touch with the others."

"No problem. Take care and be careful."

When I went back into the room I found Lisa having a lively conversation with Jorge Cortez. Valencia sat in his leather chair, following their conversation. It seemed as though Cortez was interrogating her. I had no problem with that, however, I did not want him to harass her. I just hoped that their being previously acquainted would not ruin things.

I approached Lisa, put my hand on her shoulder, and said jokingly, "I hope that Mr. Cortez is not giving you a hard time."

Lisa smiled at me.

"As you can see, I am managing just fine."

I addressed Cortez.

"I hope that you find my choice acceptable. I understand that you two have met before."

He forced a smile.

"That is correct. We do know each other, however, the young lady is not very fond of me."

Lisa responded quickly.

"How can you say that? I don't know how you came to that conclusion. It is absolutely not true."

Valencia broke his silence.

"Excuse me for interrupting this social gathering, but I suggest we use what little time we have left to organize ourselves."

Earlier, I had time to update Lisa on everything, and this time, I hadn't withheld anything. It was her life at risk and the more she knew, the better her chances were of making correct decisions. I did not have time to check if my hotel room had been turned into a recording studio and I could not take any chances at this critical stage, so we sat in a far corner of the hotel lobby. I told her about my agreement with Valencia and my suspicions about Cortez. I didn't tell her about Ricardo's team that would follow the kidnappers after the transaction.

"The most important thing," I explained over and over again, "is to stay calm. All you need to do is to see Carmen. If you get a chance, try to talk to her, calm her. Tell her that she will soon be home. If you don't get the chance to speak with her, that's fine, too. Don't insist upon it. Don't try to start a conversation with the kidnappers. Talk to them only if they talk to you. It is very important to be calm. Smile a lot. You have a conquering smile; use it and conquer. No sharp movements. Measure your movements and control them. Do almost everything in slow motion."

Lisa listened quietly, trying to remember everything. I touched her face.

"I want you to know that I will be very close behind you. Though I don't believe anything bad will happen, if anything does, I will be there within seconds. You can be sure of that."

"I will be all right," she said quietly. "You really don't have to worry, Ethan. Everything will be OK. Believe me, I'm a big girl. I will manage. You'll see, I'm good with people."

I took her hand in mine.

"Lisa, please be careful. Don't do anything uncalled for. All I am asking is that you identify the girl. That's all. And one more thing, please take this cell phone."

I gave it to her. It was similar to a phone used by many people in Mexico; however, it had a very strong, undetectable transmitter. I could hear everything that happened and they would never discover that the phone was also a listening device.

Now, she was here with me in Valencia's mansion. He was pacing restlessly by his desk, trying to occupy his time.

"The truth is that at this point, there is nothing we need to do. From now on, they call the shots," I said, shrugging my shoulders. "We need to wait for them to call us and then we'll do as they tell us. I assume they will take many precautionary measures. They will probably make us run all around town, from one pay phone to another. Once we have the exact details, all we need to do is start following Lisa at a safe distance."

I turned to Cortez.

"I assume that you have a surveillance vehicle ready for whatever we may need."

Cortez confirmed, "A special vehicle has been ready since yesterday. What do you think, should we take a photographer with us?"

"Do you mean a technician?" I reacted with indifference. "You decide. Since we are not planning to go after them anyway, it seems unnecessary, but maybe you guys need some photos if you decide to pursue these people at some future date."

Jorge Cortez's expression remained frozen, his black eyes focused on me.

"I would suggest putting a wire on the young lady, just in case."

"No, we won't," I interrupted him abruptly, "it's very dangerous. They will search her before they say a word. We can't give them any excuse to cancel the meeting. On the contrary, we need them to trust that all we want is to verify that Carmen is safe. Nothing more, nothing less."

The phone rang. Valencia looked at me.

"It's them," he said as he sat heavily in his chair. Cortez took out his cigarettes from his pocket. I took Lisa's hand and led her to the other phone extension.

"I want you to translate every word that is being said. Pick up the phone immediately after Mr. Valencia does and start listening. They cannot hear you on this phone."

Valencia reached for the phone. Cortez stood by him. I lifted my hand, "Mr. Valencia, please," and he picked up the phone.

"How is Carmen?" he asked.

"She is well. We are taking good care of her. She is homesick, but otherwise, she is fine."

"When can I see her?"

"It all depends on you. If it were up to us, she would already be home. Insisting on seeing her before you pay the money has caused unnecessary delays."

"I insist. Without that, you will not see the money."

"You are just stubborn. We can send you a Polaroid with today's paper. You make everything complicated."

"I have learned my lesson."

"That's fine; we will do it your way. As you can see, we always have the customer in mind. We hope you're not planning anything funny. If you do, it will cost you dearly. It will not help Carmen, either. If you want to receive her in one piece and not in separate bags, don't even think of playing any tricks on us."

"I told you. I gave you my word of honor that all I want is to make sure that Carmen is alive; nothing more, nothing less."

"Will you be coming yourself or will you have someone represent you?"

"No. I will not be there myself. I am sending someone else."

"Who is it? I hope for your sake and the girl's that you aren't thinking of sending the police or your security because..."

"No, no. I am sending a woman. She works in one of my companies."

"You're sending a woman?"

"Yes, so you will be sure that my intentions are pure. I want this story to have a happy ending as much as you do. When can we see Carmen? I would like it to be today."

"We appreciate that you want it to be today, but remember who is in charge. This time, it is not you. Get used to it."

"I know that you are in charge. I haven't forgotten it for a second. Set the time and place that you prefer. How long after the meeting do you want to make the exchange? I mean, the money for Carmen? Can it be on the same day?"

"Again, you are giving us instructions."

"I just want to make sure that you won't kill her 10 minutes after the meeting."

"You cannot be sure, Señor Valencia. You can't be sure. We will tell you when the exchange is going to take place. It will surely not be on the same day."

I caught Valencia's eyes and signaled him to try to ease the atmosphere and lower the tension level.

"Good. So be it," he responded.

"Great, Señor Valencia, just wonderful. I see you understand. As a reward for your good behavior, the meeting with your daughter will take place today."

"Today? When?"

"It depends on your girl. Now pay attention. I will give you exact instructions how to get to the meeting place. Listen well because I will not repeat myself. I want her to leave Mexico City and take Route 57…"

"Yes."

"Don't interrupt me. I don't want her to make a mistake that will cost Carmen's life. She is not to take the toll road, but stay on the open road, is that clear?"

"Yes."

"After the intersection with Route 150, 15 kilometers and 650 meters exactly, there is a small gas station on the right side of the road. On the left-hand side of the station, there is a pay phone. We checked it and it is working. She needs to be there at 10:30 a.m., waiting for our instructions."

"Maybe you want to do the exchange today?"

"Señor Valencia, you are playing with fire. I thought I made it clear. You will not tell us what to do. You will not decide or even suggest anything. You are very lucky that we agreed to make this meeting happen. It is only because you have the reputation of a man who keeps his word. Don't push it. We will release Carmen when we decide. We can afford waiting a day or two for the money. We are not in a rush."

"I understand."

"Now tell your girl to do exactly, and I mean *exactly*, as we tell her and everything will be OK. Remember, 10:30 a.m. by the telephone booth at the gas station on Route 57. Wait for our instructions. Is that clear? If you want to see Carmen alive, she should do exactly as she is instructed. I really hope for your sake that this woman is trustworthy."

The call ended. Valencia put the phone down and looked at Cortez.

"Where does that road lead to?"

"On both sides of Route 57, there are small agricultural villages. Eventually, it leads to the pyramid site in Teotihuacán."

"With your permission, I would like to leave and get my vehicle and men ready. Mr. Eshed, I understand that you will be riding with us?"

I nodded.

"Yes, Mr. Cortez. But I want to make it clear: We are taking one car with only one alternate car behind us—just a driver and one team only. I don't want to find more of your men out there. In the countryside, we are all very conspicuous and our presence should be kept to a minimum. I want everything to end quickly and safely with no surprises."

33.

It seemed better than I could wish for. At exactly 10:29 a.m., Lisa stopped the black Rover given to her by Valencia by the payphone at the gas station on Route 57. The weather was pleasant. The sudden rain a few hours earlier had cleaned the air. The skies were bright and the visibility was excellent. The road, a major gateway to and from the east, was busy both ways.

From our van we could see Lisa quickly exiting the Rover, walking toward the phone and picking it up. A minute later, she ran back to the car. She headed east on Route 57.

Jorge Cortez, sitting next to me in blue jeans and a very neatly pressed white shirt, ordered the driver to follow the Rover. I usually insist on driving in such sensitive situations, but this time, for the sake of avoiding confrontation, I agreed to Cortez's driver sitting behind the wheel.

"We are continuing to follow her," he said in English without looking at me.

"Make sure he keeps a safe distance. I don't want any problems," I answered.

I did not expect any problems. In the hour and a half between the phone call and the time Lisa had to leave to the first rendezvous, I had ample time to prepare for the task.

First of all, I took advantage of Cortez's departure to plant a GPS transmitter on the Rover's left fender. This gadget was supposed to let Miguel, in the van, know Lisa's exact location at any time.

At the last minute, I decided to divide my forces to allow for maximum coverage. I asked Alejandro and Ricardo to rent two cars and position themselves on Route 57, a few hundred yards from each other. They would be dispatched by cell phone according to the signals received from Lisa's vehicle. I hoped that at least one of them would be able to pick up the kidnappers' car leaving the meeting point.

"I really hope that your girl can stand the pressure. It looks like they are going to make her drive through half of Mexico," said Cortez.

"She will be fine. Don't worry. I trust her."

Through the front windshield, I saw Lisa driving over 60, passing cars like a skilled racecar driver.

"Carlos," I heard Cortez warn his driver, "don't lose her."

A few minutes later, we passed a Subaru parked at the side of the road with its hood up. Behind the car I spotted Ricardo having a heated discussion with a young woman I did not recognize. I did not turn my head back to look at them as we passed them by.

Two police cars with wailing sirens passed us in a hurry.

"I think we should slow down a little," I told Cortez. "The last thing we need is to be stopped for speeding."

I barely finished the sentence when another police car

passed us. This was one car too many to be a coincidence. What the hell was happening?

"The place is full of police," I said to Cortez. "Do you have a clue as to what's happening?"

I immediately suspected that all these cops had something to do with us being here. Maybe the kidnappers had spotted us and decided to let the police take care of us.

Cortez continued facing forward and did not reply. I think he enjoyed my anxiety. Familiar fears came back to me. What is he up to now? What is his game?

Eventually he said, "Don't mind them. There is nothing to worry about. It's a show they put on, usually to impress tourists."

For a second I lost sight of Lisa, but the Rover reappeared a few seconds later. Cortez whispered something to the driver. From his hand gestures, I understood that he asked him to slow down a little.

"This is the reason for this police fest," he said as he pointed toward a Toyota 4X4 with a California license plate that had flipped over. Two patrol cars were parked in the front and back of the vehicle. Two young men, apparently tourists, were arguing with three police officers.

"This is going to cost them dearly," laughed Cortez. "They are going to pay a lot of money for this accident. Our policemen wait for these things to happen. They can already smell dollars."

I saw Alejandro in front of a BMW parked in a gas station studying a map.

Our driver yelled something in Spanish. I didn't need translation to understand him. I could see Lisa leaving the main road and entering a side street.

"Tell him to slow down," I told Cortez quickly. "Tell him to slow down and go after her slowly, but not to continue on the side street."

Cortez translated my instructions. His eyes were also set on the scene ahead.

"These people are no fools," he said. "They are going to make her drive from village to village. It is not going to be that easy."

Our van came to a stop by the side of the road. The driver asked Cortez something—a question he did not bother to answer. He looked very tense.

"We are too exposed here. Where is the alternate vehicle?" I asked.

He did not reply, instead he started yelling into his radio.

"What happened?" I asked.

"When you go to sleep with children, don't be surprised if you wake up wet," he answered nervously. "They are stuck three kilometers behind us. They were supposed to...never mind. No use getting all worked up about this now."

Far ahead, we could see the Rover leave the paved road and enter a dirt road. We exchanged looks.

"Where are they leading her?" I asked him.

Cortez looked around. "I have no clue. I have never been in this area. I am beginning to regret this whole thing. I suggest we stop here. If we continue, they will definitely notice us. We really are too exposed."

"We will go in a little further and stop," I said. "Do you have some powerful binoculars?"

We stopped a few hundred yards from the point where Lisa had left the road. Cortez was already holding two black leather cases. He handed one of them to me.

"To tell you the truth, Mr. Eshed, I have a bad feeling about this. What is happening here is so far from what I envisioned. It seems that they are not stupid at all."

I took the case from him. To some degree, I enjoyed his show of incompetence and the nonprofessional behavior of his team. If worse came to worst, I could always blame him for this operational failure.

I thought about my team, Miguel, Ricardo and Alejandro, and how we could have done better if only we had been able to act freely. I didn't know where they were at this moment. I hoped the GPS transmitter was working and that Miguel kept them somehow on Lisa's tail.

34.

Everything that could go wrong did.

What seemed at first to be a "piece of cake" had turned into a total fiasco. It started with the alternate vehicle, which was supposed to allow us to continue our way without the kidnappers spotting us, getting stuck behind us.

When it finally arrived 10 minutes later, we ran to it. Lisa was nowhere to be found. We drove around the dirt roads like rats in a maze, but could find nothing.

Cortez was furious. The man who always kept his poise was losing it. He was shouting into his radio, giving orders, threatening his own people, yelling at the driver and making numerous calls on his cell phone.

In a desperate attempt to locate the Rover, he called in all his troops. Within minutes no fewer than 20 vehicles were patrolling the area. It was no use telling Cortez that if the kidnappers had not noticed us before, now they would have to be totally blind not to see the frantic activity he created. If they were looking for an excuse to break contact with us, we gave them a very good one. It was no use telling him this because the way things were going, and the way he was reacting, he would not have listened to reason. Every comment I could have made would've made things worse.

He called the search parties over and over again to regain his dignity, but to no avail.

"I have *never* had something like this happen to me!" he yelled with extreme frustration. "Someone is going to pay dearly for this," he told me.

We were not too far from the crowded metropolitan area of Mexico City, but this place seemed as though it were on a different planet. It took me back to my military days when we were going in and out of the run-down refugee camps of the Gaza Strip.

There were no paved roads. All the roads were narrow dirt trails more suited for a mule or a mountain goat than for a motor vehicle. The houses were made out of clay with an occasional tin wall or roof. It was an unbelievable contrast to the riches of the urban center not so far away.

Men and women in ragged clothes and large sombreros walked the road with frozen expressions. Children, barefoot and dirty, waved at us as they ran near the cars.

On one hand, I was very frustrated that I would not be able to fulfill my promise to Lisa. If something happened, I would not be there to help her. On the other hand, watching Cortez fail gave me extreme, though cruel, pleasure.

I could have helped him with one phone call to Miguel, who would have told me where she was at this exact moment; however, I had no interest in doing so. I didn't want Cortez to save face, and more important, I didn't want to expose my team and my secret plan.

Only half an hour later, when Cortez went to confer with one of his top aides, did I have a chance to call

Miguel.

"Hi, tell me quickly what's happening," I said skipping the regular niceties.

His voice was very calm.

"Everything looks one hundred percent. Alejandro is on her tail right now. Every once in a while we are rotating positions, like we agreed upon."

"Where is she now?"

"A few minutes ago she got back on Route 57. My guess is that she is going to Teotihuacán…"

I interrupted him.

"Miguel, please tell Alejandro and Ricardo not to lose her—at least one of them. We did. Can you hear me? We lost her, and I need you to cover her during the meeting. Tell them that I am stuck here and you guys are responsible for her. I don't want anything to happen to her, do you understand? If something goes wrong, you have authority to act."

"Understood. If you want, I can tell you where she is exactly."

"No. No need for that right now. Just make sure she is covered. I don't want anything to happen to her. I repeat if you need to act, do so. If you need to extract her, then do it."

"I will tell this to the guys. Don't worry, Ethan. Everything is going to be hunky-dory. I will call you."

"Don't call me. I will call you. You never know who will be with me. I will call when I can."

Around 1:00 p.m., I took advantage of Cortez leaving to speak with his chief of security, by calling Miguel again.

"Everything is under control," he answered in a monotonous tone. "Ricardo is not too far away from her. They are in this archeological site, near a place called *"Calle de Los Muertos"*—"The Avenue of the Dead"—how appropriate. I think that this is where it will take place."

"How is she acting?" I asked worried.

"She's fine. She responds quickly and has met all their deadlines. She had some problem with the car a few minutes ago, but she recovered from it. She is really good."

Around 2:00 p.m., as Cortez and I were considering whether we should continue our search in this area or go back to Mexico City, he got a call saying that the Rover was spotted in Teotihuacán.

"Finally," he sighed. "I hope the meeting hasn't taken place yet."

Half an hour later, we entered through the site's northern entrance. Cortez gave his people instructions and I went to the gift shop nearby to purchase a map of the place. Now, I not only marveled at the sights, but also educated myself about the history of the place. I already knew that our business here was done, so I might as well enjoy the scenery.

I had been to many archeological sites in Europe, the Far East and in the Middle East, but this place was one of the most impressive ones I had ever visited. Although preoccupied with Lisa's safety, I still had the presence of mind to absorb the magic and ancient beauty of the place.

Despite the heat and sun, many tourists were walking the main path, the "*Calle de Los Muertos*," from the citadel to the 12 structures in the compound.

From the minute we parked our car, Cortez had ignored my presence. I was not offended. On the contrary, it gave me time to study the remarkable structures, including the tallest one: the impressive Sun Pyramid.

Twice a year, the sun is located directly above it. Another structure's walls were decorated with 365 images of snakes, for the number of days in a year. Then there was the Palace of the Jaguars, the Palace of the Snails, and the Pyramid of the Moon linking Teotihuacán to the seat of one of the gods.

When we got to "*Plaza de la Luna*" at the end of "*Calle de Los Muertos*," I got another chance to call Miguel.

"I'm on the kidnappers' tail," he said.

"Where's the girl?" I asked.

"She should be on her way back to Mexico City. You don't have to worry about her. She's a little thing with big balls."

"Where are you now?"

"We're back in the rural area. I am really on top of them; they are in a white station wagon that barely moves—a man and a woman. The man is driving and the woman is in the back with the child. Alejandro is a kilometer or two ahead and Ricardo is behind me."

"Excellent. Now tell me about the meeting. Where did it take place? What happened there? How was the girl?"

Miguel was silent for a moment. "It was about 15 minutes ago, maybe a little more, in the palace area. The whole thing took no longer than five minutes."

"Did she see the child?"

"Yes, sure. I have pictures of everything if you want. The woman was very confident. She approached the kidnappers as though they had been friends forever. She smiled a lot and the meeting could have easily been mistaken for a family reunion, but she is a lot prettier than them."

"You're very funny," I said without laughing. "Where are you now?"

"We are going back the same way. The general direction is toward Mexico City, but I think their destination is one of the small villages in the area. Ricardo is on them now, do you want him to call you?"

"No, just don't lose them, and don't do anything without my authorization—no private initiatives. When they stop, take your positions and wait for my instructions. Is that clear?"

"No problem."

But the problems came in no time. Just 20 minutes later, Cortez and his people were canvassing the area including the banks of the San Juan River that crosses the southern side of the site trying to find I don't know what. Then my phone rang. The fact that Miguel called in spite of my explicit instructions could mean only one thing: bad news.

"What happened?" I asked trying to avoid Cortez's curious stare and at the same time, stay calm while my insides were burning with anxiety.

"I can't hear you; speak up."

"I don't know how it happened, but we lost them. I really...I don't...Alejandro was supposed to..."

I interrupted him.

"I understand Miguel, thank you." The last thing I wanted is for Cortez to find out that I had a team of my own and that we, like he and his men, failed to locate the kidnappers' hiding place.

"Let me see what I can do and I will get back to you later." I didn't wait for his answer before I hung up. Cortez looked forward, but I can swear I saw a little smile on his sleazy face.

"So, what are we going to do now?" I asked trying to divert his attention from my phone conversation. "I think it is clear that we lost them. In my opinion, there is no use staying here."

"You're right," said Cortez. "It seems like we are chasing the wind."

35.

The disgust I felt toward Cortez and his men following their shameful performance turned into utter frustration when I learned that we had also screwed up. How could I face Valencia and tell him that we were so close yet we blew it?

In the meantime, my only comfort was seeing Cortez being humiliated in front of his father-in-law, trying to find excuses, and blame the failure on his subordinates.

"I will fire every one of them! They do not deserve to call themselves security professionals. No one has ever humiliated me professionally like these people did today."

Valencia looked at him without saying a word. He was very angry and it showed.

I left them and went to look for Lisa. I was told that the first thing she asked for when she arrived was to take a shower. Valencia immediately offered her one of his many guest rooms to freshen up.

I knocked on her door, and she told me to come in. She came toward me, beautiful and glamorous, taking a bite from a big apple that she held in her hand.

"I am so hungry," she said, smiling. "I could eat anything that crosses my path, so be careful, very careful," she said with a teasing expression. "I didn't have anything to eat today, and in Mexico, skipping a meal is a serious crime."

I pulled her toward me.

"How was it?" I asked, my arms wrapped around her waist tightly. "My people told me you acted like a pro. So tell me everything."

Lisa got loose from my grip.

"I think it was good," she answered cautiously. "It was a lot faster than I thought it would be. It took no more than five minutes. The girl looked very scared. She barely said a word, but she looked OK. I mean she is not hurt or bruised or anything like that."

"And the man and woman—how did they act?"

"Nothing special. The woman seemed edgy. She stayed in the car with the girl. The man was actually very nice. He was very excited."

"Did you speak with him?"

Lisa smiled, embarrassed somewhat.

"He couldn't take his eyes off me. I don't know who or what he was expecting, but it surely wasn't someone like me."

"Did he say anything?"

Lisa thought for a moment as she reclined sensually on the leather couch situated in the middle of the room.

"He asked me if we really intended to pay the ransom or if this was all one big charade. He also asked if the insurance company was involved and if they are the ones paying the money. I could see on his face that he was afraid and tired. The woman—I think that she was the one in charge—yelled at him not to speak to me. She was holding a gun and she kept it aimed at the little girl. Poor little Carmen! She was very nervous and I was afraid she would shoot the girl by accident. The girl was blindfolded and the two kidnappers wore large sunglasses and baseball caps. I understand that this is important, isn't it?"

Indeed it was. I breathed a sigh of relief when she told me that Carmen was blindfolded. That fact alone told me that they intended to release her. If they had intended to kill her anyway, they wouldn't care if she could recognize them or not.

I sat next to her on the sofa and gently put my hand on her shoulder.

"You did a great job," I told her, enjoying feeling her silky skin. "I really can't thank you enough. From what I heard, you handled yourself as though you have done this a dozen times."

Lisa cuddled in my arms like a little girl. She put her head on my chest and closed her eyes.

"I'm glad I could help you," she said.

I moved her head toward mine and kissed her lips.

"Who knows, maybe one day I will surprise you and come to your office in Los Angeles. Maybe I will finally take my sister's advice."

I didn't say a word. I didn't know what to say. My thinking moved from the beautiful woman in my arms and her promise to the situation at hand.

I had to find a way out of this dead end I was in. This crazy gamble, to meet with them face to face was our best and only chance to get closer to their hiding place, and it backfired. We were probably in a worse position than before the meeting. The minute my team lost the kidnapers, we lost the upper hand.

The more I thought about the odds, the more my sense of failure deepened. It was all lost, forever. The one-time opportunity on which we had put all our chips did not pan out. It all went down the drain.

The only decent thing to do at this stage of the game

was to face Valencia, admit my failure and let him do as Cortez had advised him all along: pay the money and hope for the best. The horrifying statistic that only 30 percent of kidnapping incidents in Mexico end up with the victim surviving lingered in my head.

My fingers played with Lisa's hair as I tried to think about what I was going to say to Valencia in a few minutes.

"So, what happens now?" Lisa asked softly. "What are we going to do now? What's our next move?"

"There is not much we can do," I sighed heavily. "I have no good news. My people screwed up and all we did...I mean, all you did was for nothing."

Suddenly Lisa sat up.

"What do you mean?"

"I mean exactly what I said. I had people follow you all the way to the meeting and then, once you left, they followed the kidnappers. That is, until they lost them somewhere in all those damn villages. Mr. Valencia does not know of this yet, but I plainly and simply failed."

She finally grasped the seriousness of the situation.

She stood up, all worked up, and cried, "I don't believe it! You are trying to tell me that we were not able to find them? I did all this for nothing? How could a thing like this happen?"

"I still don't have all the details about how it all happened. All I know is that it did. My men followed them for a while, in three cars, and then they suddenly disappeared."

I looked at her, ashamed. I understood her frustration and felt for her.

"I think the only thing we can do now is pay the ransom and pray for Carmen's safe return. I don't know how I can stand in front of Valencia with this news."

Lisa smiled to herself.

"You remember I told you that the guy, the kidnapper, started to flirt with me?" she started with hesitation, but gained confidence as she went along. "It was very important to him that I did not think of him as a bad person, as opposed to the woman, his partner. He even said that if he had known how it was going to be, he would not have gotten involved in the whole thing. He said his cut is pathetic. He is not going to make a lot of money for this job. I think that this is his first time and that he is not very comfortable with this whole ordeal. He felt very out of place and given a second chance, he would not have made the same decisions he made this time around."

Lisa stopped for a moment, trying to guess what my reaction would be to what she was about to tell me.

"I don't know how we got to it, but I told him that I would make sure he gets much more money than he is getting now. I don't know why I even said that."

She was silent again. Since I only listened to her without responding, her hesitation grew.

"To make a long story short, I gave him my phone number and I told him that I could help him if he was interested."

I almost jumped out of my chair.

"You gave him your phone number?!" I asked in shock. "I can't understand this. What made you give him your phone number?"

"I don't know. I did it without thinking, out of instinct. I thought maybe we could lure him to our side. I told him that there was a reward of $1.5 million for anyone who could provide information leading to the safe release of Carmen."

What seemed at first to be a reckless and stupid act started shaping up as a genius move that might just be the one way to break the whole thing open. I was about to regain my self-esteem and it was all due to an incredibly bold, intuitive and unselfish risk that Lisa took.

"Did the woman notice that you gave him the note? What was his response? Did he say anything?"

Lisa smiled at me with relief, as she shook her head.

"I was very afraid to tell you this part. I thought you would be extremely angry with me. I just noticed he was under so much pressure that I wanted to break the ice a little bit. I know it was irresponsible. You're not mad at me, Ethan, are you?"

I hugged her and caressed her face gently.

"To be honest, I don't know whether to kiss you or be angry with you. You took an unnecessary risk. When this whole thing is over, he may try to find you. You don't even know who he is, what kind of person he is, or what trouble he could cause you..."

Lisa interrupted me.

"But maybe he will call today, or maybe tomorrow. Maybe he will figure out that I gave him a way out of the mess he's in. I have a strong feeling that I will hear from him again very soon. You should have seen his eyes when I gave him the note."

"You are absolutely sure that his partner didn't see anything or suspect anything?"

"She couldn't see anything. She was in the car holding the girl. You're not angry, right?"

How could I be angry with her? She had just given me life and restored my hope. I knew that the chance that he would call was slim, but still it was a chance I did not have 30 seconds ago. There might still be a happy ending to this story, at least for our side.

"Which phone number did you give him, your home or the cell?"

"I gave him the cell number, of course. I figured that if things go wrong, I can always change it."

36.

The renewed chance at locating the kidnappers made me change what I was about to tell Valencia. I decided not to tell him about my team's failure. This affair was not over yet, and I needed them around for the final showdown if there was one. My number-one priority was keeping Valencia's spirits up. I needed him to be strong and optimistic. I wanted to believe, for him and for myself, that eventually everything would be all right.

Lisa had the same opinion.

"Wait with what you were about to say to Señor Valencia. What's the rush?" She asked as I shared my plans with her. "Maybe we'll get lucky and he will call."

"Maybe we will. I hope we will." I kissed her forehead. "I'm going out for about an hour. Wait for me here."

An hour and a half later, after a brief meeting with Miguel, I was back.

I found Valencia lying on his stomach on a massage table in his office, and his personal trainer, Nate Parker, giving him a back rub. I waited for a few moments, until Parker was dismissed.

"We're on their tails," I told him, "and we are waiting

for the right opportunity to break in."

Valencia looked worried.

"What are the chances of success?" He sat up heavily. It seemed as though the massage was not enough to relieve his anxiety. He looked exhausted. The emotional ups and downs of the day he had experienced showed.

"Where are they hiding?"

"In a house on the north side of town," I answered without hesitation. "I am afraid that if we break in without proper preparation, Carmen will get hurt. We still don't know exactly how many people are inside. We are trying to gather all this intelligence before we do anything. It is better this way. It's safer for Carmen. We don't want anything to happen to her."

I felt uncomfortable giving inaccurate information to my employer. In situations like this, I always took comfort in knowing that even the Almighty when devising his Ten Commandments knew that there would be times when people would need to cut corners, and so He did not include, 'Thou shall not lie.' Still, however philosophically justified, I felt bad doing this.

"So where are they now, did you say?"

"In a neighborhood on the north side of town," I answered without blinking as I handed him the big brown envelope I held in my hand. The envelope contained the pictures Miguel took of the meeting. In only one of the pictures was Carmen's blurry image present together with the woman. The rest of the pictures were of Lisa and the male kidnapper.

Señor Valencia sat in one of the big armchairs and stared for a long time at the picture of his daughter. Thankfully, he did not ask for details as to how I got the photos. He kissed the girl in the picture. It was a touching scene. A wave of warmth and admiration toward this distinguished man filled me. He was a sensitive and emotional man with the ability to control himself when he needed to. I appreciated these qualities in a person. It occurred to me that he was the exact opposite of Cortez who was a man with no true feelings. I was proud that this was the man I was working for, and I promised myself that this time, I would not let him down.

After he looked at all the pictures, I told him about the offer Lisa made to the kidnapper. I told him that it is a long shot, but things more bizarre than this have happened.

"At this point, I don't expect him to call. However, if he does, I would rather do it this way than just storming in. As you probably know, when you go with a violent solution, you know how it is going to start, but you never know how it will end. Lisa figures that for the right reward, he will double-cross his comrades. Judging by my acquaintance with her, her intuitions are very reliable. I have never found her intuitions to be wrong. I think we should prepare ourselves for the chance that he will call. Can you put the money together in a few hours?"

He nodded. He was looking again at the picture of his daughter. His eyes were full of tears. I put my hand on his arm.

"Don't worry. We will get Carmen back. Now it's only a matter of hours."

"I hope so. I really hope so. Lisa told me that Carmen looked frightened. Poor child! She probably knows what kind of monsters these people are and what they are capable of doing. She knows she may die soon, poor child."

I didn't get a chance to answer him.

Lisa ran into the room, breathless, and exclaimed, "He called! He called me! He called me just a minute ago!" She looked at Valencia and then at me. "He called me a minute ago."

244 • *Angel in a Foreign City*

"What did he say?" I asked, saying a silent thank you to whatever force was on our side at this particular moment.

"He said that I should meet him at 7:00 p.m. near "The Angel"—the Independence Monument on the corner of Rio Tiber Street. He will come and pick me up in his car."

Her excitement was contagious. It sounded almost too good to be true and definitely a lot better than I could have ever imagined it to be. I took her face in my hands.

"Great job, but now you need to relax. Breathe deeply and try to recreate the phone conversation that you just had. Every single word of it, every pause, every background noise; it's all extremely important. It is critical that you remember everything that was said."

Lisa peeked at me, focused on Valencia and took a deep breath.

"We didn't talk much. The conversation was very short. Roberto—his name is Roberto—or at least that was how he introduced himself, asked if I was serious about the reward, about the 1.5 million dollars. I told him, 'yes, this is what the Señor offered.' He said that we needed to do this right away because his friends want to do the exchange tomorrow morning, early in the morning. I think he was calling from a pay phone or something like that because there was a lot of noise and traffic in the background."

I saw Valencia become very alert.

"They really want to do it tomorrow? Nobody has called yet to give us any information or instructions. I haven't heard anything from them."

"How is the meeting going to take place? How are we going to get the information?" I asked.

"He told me to wait for him by the monument at 7:00 p.m. exactly. He will be driving a green VW Bug, like the ones used as taxis. He will pick me up. He asked if he could trust that I would not turn him in to the police. I told him that if he didn't believe me, he could speak directly with Señor Valencia himself. He said that my word was enough for him."

"And what was your agreement about the money?"

At this point, Lisa was a little hesitant.

"I hope I didn't step beyond the boundaries here, but I had to say something otherwise he would have changed his mind. I told him that he could get a third of the money tonight, half a million dollars, and the rest of it when Carmen is safely back home. I hope it's all right. I had no one to ask...I..."

Valencia walked over to her.

"You did well Lisa." He hugged her and kissed her on her cheek. "Thank you. You are a very good person, a very good child."

Lisa smiled.

"You think so, too, Ethan?" she asked nervously.

"Yes, I do," I assured her. "You did exactly what you were supposed to do and even better. I am sure that in a past life you were a police detective. You are thinking and reacting just like a professional. Now where is this monument?"

"*El Angel*," she said assuming the role and tone of a tour guide, "is a monument of an angel with wings made of pure gold. It is on top of a tall column and was erected in 1910 in commemoration of the Mexican Day of Independence from the Spanish: September 16, 1810..."

Señor Valencia cut short Lisa's speech.

"With your permission, I must go take care of the money. How much do you need? A million and a half dollars?"

"Yes, Señor Valencia," she replied, "but only half a million tonight."

"Did he specify the kind of bills he wanted?"

"No, he didn't," Lisa answered. "He was so nervous that he didn't even think about that."

At that exact moment, the phone rang. Valencia reached for the phone with a quick movement.

"Sí. Sí, Señor Valencia, sí," he fired rapidly.

He looked at me and from his expression, I knew exactly who was on the other line. They spoke for approximately three minutes with Valencia doing very little of the talking. Whenever he responded, he was incredibly relaxed and confident.

When he finally put down the phone, he sat down in his chair and repeated the instructions he was just given in a mechanical tone.

"The trade will take place in two steps. Payment will be made first, and then they will tell me where I can find Carmen. When I asked them to do it simultaneously saying that this is the fair way to carry out the transaction, they answered harshly that my time to decide the terms for them was over. From now on, they will be the ones who decide everything and if this is not acceptable, I can forget about Carmen. First, I have to turn over the money, and only then will they call me with the location." He looked me straight in the eye, "They do not suspect anything."

"That is exactly what Roberto said," commented Lisa. "It's a sign that he was not lying."

"Did he say where they want the money?" I asked.

"All he said is that I needed to have the money ready. They would call an hour ahead of time and tell me where. Do you think I can trust them, Ethan? I am worried that they will take the money and kill Carmen. I…"

"I hope it won't come to that. We have an excellent chance of finishing this whole thing tonight, before you have to make the payment."

37.

At exactly 6:57 p.m., Lisa was standing on Rio Tiber Street by the golden angel.

From the driver's seat of the Rover, the same one that Lisa had used earlier today, I could see Lisa leaning on a post. The duffle bag with half a million dollars was at her feet.

If she was nervous or excited, it did not show. She looked so casual and poised that one might think that this was a routine situation for her.

"I love that girl," said Valencia who was sitting beside me in the Rover. "I know that she is not expecting anything in return, but I assure you that I will take care of her for the rest of her life, as if she were my own daughter."

His words touched me and relieved me. I was very concerned about Lisa's well-being after all this was over. I had my doubts about going ahead with this plan. Too many uncertainties and not enough control always made for a dubious outcome. The risk of sending her out into the night with no experience, no knowledge of whom she was about to deal with, no foolproof, reliable backup and half a million dollars in cash was tremendous. What if this

Roberto was not as she had felt he was? What if after taking the money he killed her and ran away without telling us where his friends are? With so many variables, there were multiple things that could go wrong.

One thing that really worried me was the haste with which they agreed to things. The details were not entirely worked out. What if he felt he had no assurance that the rest of the money would be paid to him after Carmen was rescued? What if his friends suspected him as he left the hiding place to pick up Lisa? So many 'what if' questions.

Despite my serious apprehensions, I had to give my blessing to the plan. It was the last and only chance we had to bring Carmen back under our terms. It was my only chance to maintain my personal reputation and prove that I was indeed worthy of the trust Valencia and Rob placed in me. Lisa insisted upon going, she did not even let me finish the sentence when I asked her to reconsider.

The decision to allow Valencia to join me in the backup vehicle was also agonizing. Both professional and selfish considerations were involved. I needed someone to translate the conversation between Lisa and Roberto. I didn't want to use Cortez or his people, and I didn't want to expose any of mine. The only other person that could fill this position was Valencia. Since he insisted upon joining me, I agreed.

I used the time between the call and the meeting to put as many precautionary measures in place as I could. I wanted to be ready to react effectively to as many developing scenarios as possible. In the liner of the bag Lisa was carrying, I planted an additional powerful transmitter in the unlikely event that the cell phone transmitter did not work. It was based on a relatively new technology that was superior, but not totally reliable. This was a life-and-death situation, and there had to be backup for everything. I had a conference call with Miguel, Alejandro and Ricardo. They would be positioned in the meeting area, ready for action and awaiting my instructions. The Rover still had the GPS tracker, and so did Lisa's duffle bag. There was no way we were going to lose them this time. I figured that it would not be long until we knew if we were on track. This was not something that would require patience. It would call for determination and fast action. I made my team aware of my concerns, and they agreed.

At 7:02 p.m., a green VW Bug stopped next to Lisa. I saw her pick up her duffle bag and get into the car. The car sprinted ahead, and I was behind it.

In the small speaker, I heard them clearly. Valencia translated every word.

"I hope that you will not try to play games with me. I hope this is not the biggest mistake of my miserable life. If my partners found out about this, they would kill me—no question about that. Did you bring the money?"

"Yes, Roberto. Relax. All the money is here—half a million dollars, just as we agreed."

There were a few seconds of silence until the man's voice was heard,

"Let's finish this quickly. I want to get back to my friends before they start suspecting anything. As you know, they tend to be paranoid at times. They have already called Valencia and told him that they want the money tomorrow."

"How many are you, Roberto?"

"Five. I joined after they already took the girl. My uncle owns the building she is being kept in. He got me in on this. I didn't even take part in the kidnapping itself."

"Roberto, the money is here, but you will get it only if you tell me exactly where you are holding Carmen."

"I will tell you. Don't worry. Now, you tell me, when do I get the rest of the money and how can I be sure you will pay me?"

"Señor Valencia is a man of his word. He will keep his promise. Don't worry about that, and anyway, the money I am going to give you today is probably one hundred times more than you would have gotten from those whom you call friends. With this money alone, you can fly to America in a private jet full of beauty queens."

Roberto giggled.

"You are something special, believe me. You have an answer for every question. What you said about the money is very true. So do you think that we could have some fun together, you and I? You should! Look at me: I'm a rich boy now."

Valencia was red with anger.

"Son of a bitch! He thinks he is going to party with my money! Scum!"

I smiled. I had the feeling that what really hurt him was not the thought of that punk, Roberto, having a good time with his money, but to think of the idea that our angel, Lisa, would ever be involved with such a lowlife.

"You still haven't told me where the girl is." Lisa's voice was carried clearly over the speaker. "It's not fair. I held up my end of the bargain. I met you with the money and all you can think of is having fun. You have got to earn your money first. Where are you holding the girl?"

"It's in the northern industrial zone, behind the big supermarket. There is a big parking lot with a structure."

My eyes were focused on the VW in front of me. It didn't look as though he was aware of the possibility that someone was following him. Maybe it was Lisa's charm that made him abandon even basic instincts in a situation like this. Suddenly, he left the main road and started making his way along the narrow roads of the slums. I didn't know the place, and I was afraid to lose them. The sun was down, and the roads had become dark. Maneuvering through them was a very difficult task.

"Roberto," said Lisa, "you will not get the money unless you give me an exact address. Don't try to be smart. You won't get a dollar."

"But I don't have an exact address. Why can't you understand this? Maybe that is why they chose the place to begin with. It doesn't have an address. It is a building that stands on the edge of the parking lot of the big supermarket in the northern industrial zone. It's a two-story building. That's the most accurate address anyone can give you."

"Hold on, aren't we there? Isn't this the northern industrial zone?"

"Great, sweetheart. I see you know your way around."

"So where is it? There are a few supermarkets here. Which one are we talking about? What's the name of your big supermarket?"

"It is called 'Around the Clock,' and it's located just next to the 'Kukulos' nightclub. You know the place? Well, it's there."

"I'm not sure I'll be able to find it by myself," said Lisa. "Take me there. It's not far away."

"Why couldn't you find it? Behind the store, the supermarket, there is a parking lot. On the other side, there is a building. The girl is on the second floor and that's it."

"Show me where it is. You're not afraid, are you? If you really want to go out with me, you have to show me you trust me."

His laughter sounded nervous.

"I don't even trust myself fully. Didn't your father teach

you not to trust strangers? You look like a nice girl, but I'm sure you are sly and cunning like all the others. How are you connected to Señor Valencia anyway? Are you his lover? I heard he likes his women young."

Valencia, who translated every word, did not censor this piece, although he did call Roberto "scum," amongst other compliments during the evening. Suddenly, the VW stopped in front of an entrance to a shopping center.

"We are going into this structure and I will drop you off in the lower level and drive away. If you want, you can take it from there. It is a two-minute walk from here."

He started driving slowly into the building. To avoid being seen, I slowed down allowing for the distance between the two cars to grow.

Suddenly, a blue Citroen passed me aggressively on the right. I saw the VW disappear as it entered the building. The blue Citroen was headed toward the same entrance.

38.

Then it hit me. The Citroen was after Lisa. I wanted to kick myself for not realizing it immediately. Maybe it was the way they passed me, or the determination they showed. I didn't see the faces inside, but all the signs were there.

Were Roberto's friends inside the car? Was this a trap they planned together with Roberto, or was it just his stupidity that had gotten him caught? It didn't really matter now. Lisa was in danger.

I charged the vehicle into the garage trying to catch up with the two cars that were already out of my sight.

Valencia looked at me and asked, "What happened, Ethan?"

I didn't answer. I focused on driving down into the poorly lit parking garage. A white van heading toward us from the opposite side was thrown into the divider trying to avoid collision with the Rover. I cussed in Hebrew and accelerated. I was now able to see the blue Citroen. It, too, was gaining speed like a sports car on a racetrack.

There was no audio coming from Lisa's car and that caused me to worry more. It could have been that Roberto had found the transmitter and neutralized it, but it was very unlikely. It was either a technical malfunction or transmitting problems in an underground location, or...I didn't want to think of the other possibility.

At least it had helped us hear Carmen's exact location and we could act to get her out of there.

Now I saw the VW. Roberto had figured out that he was being chased and tried to escape his friends. He reached the bottom of the structure and was going back up the exit ramps on the opposite side. Passing under the light, I could see three people in the Citroen: a driver and two pistol-waving passengers.

The only positive thing I could think of at this moment was that if four gang members are here, then only the woman was with Carmen. It would make saving her a lot easier if we were able to contain the situation here.

I felt my stomach sink. Was it Roberto's behavior that made them suspicious when he told them he was leaving for a while? Did they follow him to his rendezvous with Lisa, or was it only a freak coincidence that they bumped into him driving with a woman—with Lisa—so close to the hiding place.

They probably recognized Lisa's face. I figured that they had people taking pictures of the meeting in Teotihuacán just as I had. Once they saw her with Roberto, they knew what had happened. It didn't take a genius to figure this one out.

It was of no real importance how they found out about Roberto's treason. They did, and now Lisa was caught in the crossfire. Roberto was a dead man. There was no doubt what the people in the blue Citroen would do to him once they caught up with him. Lisa was guilty by association. Their fate was entwined and it was up to me to try to untangle it.

I reevaluated the situation. I was determined to

continue the chase and save Lisa, but I knew I needed help. Should I call Miguel, Alejandro and Ricardo to help me here? I decided it was not a good idea. It would take too much time. They should take advantage of the fact that Carmen was alone with the woman kidnapper and get her.

Driving after the two cars like a maniac, I reached two strategic decisions. The first: Send my team to get Carmen. The second: Call the police to this location. It was my policy not to have the police involved; however, I understood that at this point, I had no other alternative. They could get here the fastest. I knew Valencia would agree.

I pushed the accelerator down hard and gave my cell phone to Valencia.

"Please call the number 310-276-7682!" I shouted. "Speak to Miguel—you can speak with him in Spanish. Tell him exactly where Carmen is. Tell him that she is probably with one woman, but they need to be careful and I authorize them to break in. Is that clear?"

Valencia, pale, did exactly what I asked him to do. In the meantime, Roberto led the chase back to the lower level. At the last second, I spotted a car trying to back out of its parking space. With an instinctive response, I broke to the right trying to avoid the car on the left and the wall on the right. The bang from the right rear told me that I was partially successful. The collision with the wall threw us skidding to the left and into harm's way. I hit the breaks but it felt like it took forever for the car to stop. We were still running.

"Are you OK?" I asked Valencia who was concentrating on talking to Miguel and did not see what had happened.

I stepped on it and reentered the chase. In two or three seconds, I was back behind the Citroen. At the next turn, I saw the green VW. Roberto was a skillful driver, but I knew it could not last forever. A car in his path, a pedestrian or an obstacle might force him to slow down and the Citroen would get him. Sooner or later, they would reach him. Their car was better and faster than Ricardo's. If you added the fact that it is always easier to follow than to lead, and that a gun bullet is faster than a driving car, his chances to out drive his former partners were nil. This did not look good; disaster was in the air.

Finally, Valencia finished giving Miguel all of my instructions.

"Do you know anyone in the police who you can really trust?" I shouted without taking my sight off the car in front of me.

"I know all of them. What do you need?"

"Call someone you trust and get them over here immediately. Tell them exactly where we are and what is happening. Tell them that we are in the Rover and the VW. Make sure they don't start shooting at us or at Lisa. The bad guys are in the Citroen. This thing here is getting out of control. I am very worried for Lisa. They need to get here fast."

Valencia stared at me.

"Do you think that the people in the Citroen…"

I didn't get to hear the end of his question. Out of nowhere, a car was coming straight on a collision course with us. Somehow, I swerved out of the car's path. Luckily, I was able to maintain control over the vehicle and the damage was minimal.

"Señor!" I yelled. "Call the police! We have no time! I need help immediately!"

We heard two shots clearly. We could not see who the shooter was or who got shot, but to me it was clear. The gang in the blue Citroen had caught up with Roberto and

Lisa, and had shot at them.

Valencia froze for a second and then revived himself, frantically pushing numbers on the cell phone. Two more shots were fired and then we heard a loud bang. My heart sank. I hurried to the lower level fearing the worst.

The scene was horrific. In the middle of the parking lot smashed against a wide concrete pillar that supported the upper deck was Roberto's green VW Bug. It was turned over on its roof. Heavy smoke left no room for doubt; Roberto had lost control of the car at high speed, hit the pillar in front of him with tremendous force and the vehicle had flipped over.

Fifty feet from the car stood the Citroen. Two young men came out of the car and started making their way toward the smashed VW, guns in hand. They wanted to make sure the job was done. My urge to stop them from getting there was stronger than my fear of the overturned car exploding. I had to get there before they did.

At that moment, I knew I was going into a shootout, and even if I did survive it, it would probably result in full or partial deafness. I hated indoor gun battles. As a police officer, I did everything to avoid them. Those few times I was forced to shoot out of a car, or in closed quarters, had left me with irreversible damage to my hearing.

I stopped the Rover with a screech of breaks near the VW. I drew the gun that was hidden under the seat. I saw that Valencia had finished the phone call to the police.

"Stay low and be careful! Don't move! Stay in the car!" I yelled at him and headed with great fear, not for myself but for Lisa, toward the smoking car.

Through the thick smoke that filled the car, I could see the two figures, Lisa and Roberto lying there motionless by each other. Ignoring everything, I reached for Lisa's hands and tried to pull her out of the wreckage.

"Lisa!" I cried as I saw her face, covered with blood. "Lisa, can you hear me? Give me a signal that you can hear me!"

The only sound I heard was two more shots that this time sounded dangerously close. I left Lisa and took cover behind the burning car. The two gunmen were getting closer quickly. The third one went into the Citroen and came out with a submachine gun.

I shot above their heads. They took to the ground with remarkable skill. They were definitely military-trained. They rolled back and took cover behind a row of cars beside them. Now, buying a few seconds, I returned to Lisa in another attempt to free her from the metal trap she was in.

Nothing worked. She was stuck in what was once the front end of a car. If only I could turn the car over, it would be much easier. I was between a rock and a hard place. If I exposed myself trying to move the car, the attackers would have a clean shot at me. That would not do Lisa or I any good.

The machine gun started blurting fire, hitting very near to me. A few bullets hit the wall behind me, spraying ricochets all over. I felt a sting in my shoulder, but I ignored it.

Suddenly, a white Toyota raced onto the scene playing very loud music. The gunman turned instinctively on his heels and started firing at the innocent intruders. The surprised driver, not knowing what hit him, tried to drive away from the shooter and crashed into a parked car. The car smashed with a loud boom, and fire started bursting from the engine. The music continued to play for a few more seconds, and then silenced.

I took advantage of the distraction and changed my position. Now I was flat on my stomach under the rear end of the VW. I aimed at the guy with the machine gun—a tall young man with Indian features—20 feet ahead of me. He was smiling with satisfaction as he shot all over the place. My hands were not steady. I took a deep breath and focused only on him. It worked. I pulled the trigger and shot three times. The submachine gun stopped firing as the man collapsed on the floor with a surprised expression on his face.

The other two, seeing their comrade fall, started shooting at me. They took opposing angles and started to move toward me, alternating their advancement. Seeing one guy exposed, I shot at him.

I was concentrating on the gun battle so much that I didn't notice the three squad cars rushing onto the scene. I didn't realize the cavalry had arrived until one of them came to a screeching halt a couple of yards from my face.

They called something in Spanish through their loudspeakers, and a deafening silence spread throughout the parking level that by now, looked like a war zone.

I noticed Valencia opening the door of the Rover and heading toward the police officers. I had totally forgotten about him.

39.

I sat on the emergency-exit stairs, shamelessly allowing tears to flow down my face. The pain I felt was immense and tore me from the inside. I looked at the VW that was now set right again. It was just a few minutes ago that the two dead bodies of Lisa and Roberto were extracted from the wreckage.

A medical staff had arrived at the scene in an ambulance a few seconds after the police. They attempted to perform a miracle. I stood by them and prayed for that miracle, knowing it would not come. I could not take my eyes off Lisa. Death did not diminish her beauty, not in the least.

"What a disaster! What a disaster!" I heard Valencia cry by my side. "Dear Lord, why did she deserve such a fate?"

I had no answer. What could I say? The extreme guilt I felt made it impossible for me to stand. It was as if thousands of swords were stabbing me internally, making the tortures of hell a desirable relief. I was the one directly responsible for her death. It was I—not Roberto, not the kidnappers, not Valencia or Cortez, and not even Lisa herself, who was responsible for this unnecessary carnage.

I was the one who allowed these circumstances to happen. She willingly went into this adventure having faith in my ability to keep her from harm's way. It was my need for professional redemption that brought her to this cursed parking structure and this hour of doom. One could even say that I encouraged her to go to the meeting at "The Angel." Now *my* angel was dead and I had no one to blame but myself.

With great effort, I suppressed my emotional distress and that caused agonizing pain. I felt comfort in this pain as though I was punishing myself for my role in Lisa's demise. I saw that this was only the beginning of what I was about to endure and I embraced it. A big roar of pain was building inside me. I was not yet ready to let it out. The only manifestations of my misery were the tears streaming from my eyes, uncontrolled. They defied my imposed external self-control and exposed my torment.

I watched the ambulance as it slowly left the scene— there was no need to rush. In an instant, an undeniable depression took me over. I felt so exhausted, helpless and empty.

Ten minutes ago, I still had hope. Throughout my military service and my time as a police detective, I had seen situations where severe and gruesome injuries were involved. I witnessed the unforgettably traumatic experience of a family trapped in their van after a collision with a train. I saw a friend hit straight in the stomach with a rocket. I had seen a lot of that in my lifetime, and most of these incidents had no survivors. I hoped that this time it would be different. I know the stories of miraculous recoveries. Injured people whom everyone, including the medical staff, had given up on somehow were able to cling on to life. They recovered and were able to rebuild their lives. I knew

Lisa. She was a fighter. I knew that if given only a ghost of a chance, she would fight for her own life and win.

After the two remaining kidnappers surrendered, the police turned over the smashed VW and tried to save the two people trapped inside. The body of the third kidnapper was on the floor in the middle of the staging area. It was obvious he needed no medical attention.

I looked at Lisa and my heart cried. The pain stung like acid. This is not how I wanted this story to end. When the medical crew tried to breathe life into her, I silently prayed, 'Please, please let her live.'

It didn't help. The doctor did whatever he could, but it was evident to everyone around that he was doing what he was doing as protocol and to satisfy the esteemed Señor Valencia who wanted to be sure that everything possible was being done. Lisa did not respond to anything and after a few more minutes, the doctor looked at us as he shut her eyes gently and said, "I'm very sorry. There is nothing that could have been done. She's gone."

The rest of the medical team could not look me in the eye. They packed their instruments and left me alone with the body.

My knees were shaking as I tried to stay on my feet. I felt my stomach turning, and all the air squeezed out of my lungs.

Valencia lowered his head so that no one would see his tears. I wanted to put my hand on his shoulder, but I could not move. Valencia was still holding my phone when it rang. He handed it to me.

"Yes, who is it?" I took a few steps back to get away from the others and regain my composure.

"Ethan? This is Miguel. Can you hear me?"

"Yes, I can hear you. What's the situation?"

"We've got the girl!" he shouted. "Can you hear me?

We've got the girl! Everything is all right!"

"How did it go?" I asked. I did not feel joy and his triumphant jubilation sounded strange to me. Carmen's fate was no longer a concern for me. Everything had become so worthless. Lisa was dead, and the rest of the world ceased to exist.

"It was a breeze. If you had been here, you would have been so proud of us! Like you said, she was alone with the woman who didn't even try to resist. She was in total shock when we came in! The girl is healthy and unharmed. What do you want us to do now?"

"Wait a second," I told him and dragged myself back to the group. They were looking somber as they watched the paramedics move the bodies into the ambulance. "I'm giving you Valencia. He will tell you where to take Carmen. Wait a second. Here he is."

I handed Valencia back the phone and heard myself saying in a dead, emotionless voice, "Mr. Valencia, we've got Carmen. She is alive and unharmed, where do you want us take her?"

Valencia took the phone and I started walking aimlessly in the parking lot until finally, I found myself sitting, exhausted and empty on the emergency-exit stairs.

It finally came out—the roar—loud, long and painful. It rolled and echoed in the closed space. I cried. A portion of the ocean of pain was released, but there was still the loss and the guilt.

40.

I boarded the plane, ignoring the flight attendant's welcoming smile, and took my place in one of the first rows. All I wished was to be as far away from this place as quickly as possible.

At first, I wanted to leave Mexico the day following Lisa's death. I wanted to go right away, without saying goodbye to anyone. I wanted to run away.

I stopped myself from doing that. I have never before, in any capacity that I have filled nor in my personal life, just left everything and run away. Not even in the hardest of times when I was at fault and embarrassed, did I run without facing the consequences of my actions. I wasn't about to change that now.

The last two days in Mexico were the worst of my life. I did not want to do anything, see anyone. Most of the time, I stayed in my room. I turned off my cell phone. I did not check my e-mail. I was in mourning. Even my usual antidepressant—a few shots of tequila—did not have the desired effect.

Thoughts of Lisa's death did not leave me. Over and over again, I replayed those wonderful hours we had spent together. Over and over again, the guilt crept back and filled areas of my conscience that I didn't even know existed.

I had experienced loss. I had lost brothers-in-arms, friends and loved ones. But I had never known a pain like this. The combination of the loss of a lover, the loss of a professional partner and the self-loathing of personal failure all combined into what was more pain than I imagined could exist.

The hardest part was seeing Lisa's grieving family at the mortuary. I didn't know anyone there except for her charming aunt, Babette. I greeted her with a mute nod. She replied with a sad smile.

I had no idea if any of the other family members knew who I was, or how I had been instrumental in Lisa's death. When shaking their hands and reciting the usual words of consolation, I could not look into their eyes.

The ceremony was short. A young woman just a bit older than Lisa, with very similar features, maybe her sister, delivered the eulogy. Since I did not understand a word, I took the time to look at Lisa's parents.

The mother, short and pale, and the father, broad shouldered with impressive black hair, both wore black. The woman cried throughout the ceremony. The man did not show any emotion. He held his wife's hand, caressing it gently.

I wanted so much to go to them, embrace them to my heart, and ask for their forgiveness. Most of all, I wanted to tell them how much I loved their daughter, and that her memory would be with me until my last day on this earth.

I did not have the strength to do it. I stood planted in my place a few feet behind them, looking at them with agonizing pain. Two priests in black robes led the prayer, and I struggled to hold back my tears.

"Enough, Ethan. What happened here is not your fault," Valencia tried to comfort me. He held my arm lightly.

"Stop torturing yourself. I was there too, remember? I am your witness in front of God and man that you did everything in your power to protect and guard her. Lisa went on this mission because she wanted to. She was not willing to consider doing it differently. It is not you who sent her. You did your best to be close to her all the time, making sure that nothing bad happened to her. If there was someone to blame in this, it was me. My fault is exactly as large as yours. At the same time, I could have forbidden her from going out that night. She had done more than enough to earn my love, even before that evening. Who could have known it would end this way?"

"My relationship with Lisa was not just professional," I found myself confessing to Valencia. "She was not just an employee paid to do a service. I feel that I used her. I exploited her love for me. I used her, and look at the end result. I don't know if you can understand me."

This conversation took place in the limousine as we were leaving the funeral home and returning to the mansion where Carmen's welcome-home party was being held. I did not want to participate in a party so shortly after Lisa's funeral; however, Valencia insisted, and since he was my host and a man I had learned to greatly appreciate, I could not refuse.

For a few moments, we sat in silence.

"Until I saw how deeply you reacted to Lisa's death," he said in a hesitant tone, choosing his words carefully, "I could have sworn that you didn't have a milligram of emotion in you. I was sure that you were some kind of man-machine who didn't take anything to heart. I thought that the only thing important to you was achieving your goal no matter what the consequences were. Now, when all the dust has settled, you have achieved your target, and your mission is complete..."

"And now you see how wrong you were?" I said in a broken voice. "Yes, the mission was accomplished, but at what a price? Mr. Valencia, I will tell you this honestly and I don't know what you will think of me for saying this: If I had known that this was going to be the price I'd have to pay to complete this mission, I wouldn't have done it."

I attended the Valencia family gathering and congratulated Carmen on her safe return home, but no one could force me to stay there for more than half an hour. I was a mourner in a room of celebrants, and all I wanted was to get out of there as fast as possible.

Jorge Cortez was nowhere to be seen. That surprised and intrigued me. I asked Valencia where his son-in-law was. He took my hand, looked around and pulled me to the side.

"Unfortunately, our suspicions of him turned out to be true. He is a relative, a close relative, but he will have to pay the price. On the day that you suggested that Lisa go and meet with the kidnappers to make sure that Carmen was alive, Cortez came to me with the offer that if I gave him the ransom money to deliver to the kidnappers, he would have Carmen here in an hour. He said that he was able, through one of his contacts, to be in direct communication with the kidnappers. He told me, "I guarantee that Carmen is still alive.""

I was astonished. Not only the nerve of the guy to come up with this offer that fingered him as a collaborator in the kidnapping, but also that Valencia did not let me in on this crucial information much earlier.

Valencia waited a few seconds as though to increase the suspense.

"I told him that I would give him the money as soon as Lisa confirmed that Carmen was alive. That made him furious. It was obvious that he was trying anything to prevent Lisa from going to the meeting."

He continued, "Then I called Hector. I don't know if you had the chance to meet him. He has been in my employ for many years now. He owes me his life. I won't go into details, but if it were not for me, he would either be in a cemetery or rotting in jail. Hector is the man closest to Cortez. I asked him to befriend him and he has not compromised his position with Cortez until this day."

Valencia enjoyed keeping me on the edge of my seat—or maybe it was his way of getting me to stay at the party longer.

"I asked Hector directly, no beating around the bush, how much he knew of Cortez's involvement in the abduction of Carmen. He was in shock. He swore that he didn't know anything about his involvement. He said, and I believed him, that if he had known anything, he would have come to tell me himself. I know that he is totally loyal to me. I asked him to tell me about the people with whom Cortez is in regular contact, especially those with criminal connections. I knew I was onto something when Hector mentioned the name of a high-ranking police officer, known to operate crime gangs at the same time he is catching criminals who do not belong to his organizations."

"Lucky for me," Valencia smiled, "I have some very good friends on the police force and I asked someone to check out that officer. I thought that maybe I would be able to get to the kidnappers through him. Then you came back from the meeting, Lisa made the appointment with Roberto, and your people saved Carmen without my assistance."

"The kids captured in the parking garage eventually

admitted that they worked for that police officer who confessed to his involvement and also mentioned Cortez's part in the plot. My son-in-law was supposed to get half of the money. The other half was for the policemen involved and the kidnappers. Now you can understand Cortez's eagerness to finish the whole affair as fast as possible. He saw that you were making progress and was afraid of you. You also understand now how the police were able to get to your female investigator, Gila, so quickly."

"Where is Cortez now?"

Valencia took a deep breath. The smile was gone.

"He is fine, for the time being. If you do not inquire further, then I will not need to lie to you. Let's leave it at that. At first, I didn't want to share any of this with you, but I felt that I owed it to you."

"And what will happen to the police officer?"

"He is going to pay a dear price for his corruption. He will be sorry until his last day for the most vicious of crimes: the kidnapping of a child."

The time to leave arrived.

"I'm sorry but I have to go. My flight departs in two hours."

"You are absolutely sure that you don't want to stay for a few more days as my guest and enjoy a pleasant vacation? It would do you good," he tried for the last time.

"No, thanks, I prefer to go back home immediately. I am not in the mood for a vacation. There's work to be done, bad people to catch. You know how it is, work, work and more work. Thank you again for your very generous offer."

"If anyone here should be grateful, it is I. You have made me a happy man, Ethan. Thanks to you, Carmen is back and my family is whole again. I have no words to convey my appreciation for what you have done for my family. Consider our house yours, and you are welcome here any day, any time. You are part of my family now."

Valencia, the distinguished and reserved man, hugged me sincerely. I hugged him back, and so we parted.

Two hours later, I buckled the seat belt in my chair on the Mexicana Airlines red-eye from Mexico City to Los Angeles. I had left Mexico forever.

Farewell, Elisa Rosario Hernandez—Lisa, my angel!

"Mr. Eshed, what will you have?" asked the smiling flight attendant.

"Tequila Patron," I answered. As she poured the drink, I requested, "Please, leave the bottle here."

1150193

Made in the USA